KIRK DOUGLAS

Young Heroes
of the Bible

KIRK DOUGLAS

YOUNG HEROES
of the BIBLE

A BOOK FOR FAMILY SHARING

ILLUSTRATED BY DOM LEE

SIMON & SCHUSTER BOOKS FOR YOUNG READERS

SIMON & SCHUSTER BOOKS FOR YOUNG READERS
An imprint of Simon & Schuster Children's Publishing Division
1230 Avenue of the Americas, New York, New York 10020
Text copyright © 1999 by the Bryna Company
Illustrations copyright © 1999 by Dom Lee

Book design by Anahid Hamparian
The text for this book is set in 13-point Classical Garamond
The illustrations are rendered by applying encaustic beeswax on paper, then scratching out images.
Printed and bound in the United States of America
10 9 8 7 6 5 4 3 2 1

Library of Congress Cataloging-in-Publication Data
Douglas, Kirk, 1916-
[Young heroes]
Young heroes of the bible. — 1st ed.
p.   cm.
Summary: Retells five Old Testament stories in which Abraham, Rebecca, Joseph,
Miriam, and David perform heroic deeds in their youth.
ISBN 0-689-81491-7
1. Children in the Bible—Juvenile literature. 2. Bible stories, English—O.T. [1. Bible stories—O.T. 2. Heroes.]
I. Title.   BS576.D68 1999   221.9'505—dc21   98-25718   CIP   AC

FIRST
EDITION

To all the grandchildren of the world

ALSO FOR CHILDREN
BY KIRK DOUGLAS

The Broken Mirror

KIRK DOUGLAS
YOUNG HEROES
of the BIBLE

CONTENTS

INTRODUCTION

WHEN I WAS A KID, I didn't like Sunday school. Didn't we have enough school during the week? Why did adults have to go and invent a special school to keep kids indoors on Sunday morning? I resented it.

The only good thing about it was that they didn't make us do homework, and when class was over, they gave us a cookie.

That's because Sunday school wasn't like real school. They only taught one subject—the Bible. In my hometown, Amsterdam, in upstate New York, Sunday school was held in the basement of the synagogue (if you were Jewish) or in the basement of a church (if you were Christian). But later, when I talked to the other kids, I found out we were all learning a lot of the same stuff—stories about Abraham, Isaac, Jacob, Moses, and other people that lived in biblical times, three or four thousand years ago. Boy, that is a long time ago!

The basement classroom, where I went to Sunday school every Sunday morning, seemed like a dungeon to me. I felt like a prisoner. The furnace was down there, so you'd think it would be warm, but it was always cold. Maybe the furnace wasn't working right. We sat on metal folding chairs in a semicircle. The chairs were cold too, so sometimes I sat on my hands.

The teacher, Mrs. Apple, sat in a big wooden chair with a red velvet cushion. But she stood up a lot and walked around while she was talking.

She was always lecturing us about how you had to be good and read the Bible. It was all very boring. We had a book with pictures full of people with big long beards. They were either very old, or they all hated to shave.

Now I am very old, and I hate to shave too. But I still feel like a kid. I don't know why this is. But there must be a good reason.

Actually, I have felt like a kid all my life. Maybe that's why I became an actor. When you are an actor in the movies, you get to play games; you pretend to be someone else—a cowboy or a boxer or a detective. My best friend, Burt Lancaster, was an actor too, and people said we never grew up. I didn't care—I had a lot of fun making more than eighty movies. Maybe you saw some of them.

I never made any movies about the Bible, but my friend Burt did—he made a movie called *Moses* and he pretended to be Moses. My friend Charlton Heston made a movie called *The Ten Commandments,* and he pretended to be Moses too. I was jealous. Why couldn't I be Moses? I made a movie where I pretended to be Spartacus, who lived in biblical times, but he never made it into the Bible.

Back when I went to Sunday school, I only liked one thing—stories about kids. The kids in the Bible were cool. They did great things and without any help from adults either.

When we got to those parts, I always wanted to know more and I would raise my hand and ask questions. When the teacher ignored me, I would ask anyhow. That's a good way to get into trouble. Many of my questions were never answered, and I didn't find the answers until I was old and started to read the Bible again.

When you get old, a funny thing happens. You forget the things that took place last week, but you remember with great clarity the things that happened many years ago, when you were a kid.

I'm remembering now all the things I learned in Sunday school, and I have to admit, there's a lot of good stuff in the Bible that isn't at all boring. In this book, I am going to retell some of my favorite stories.

I promise to leave out anything that's really dull. You won't read about old men with long beards here! In all my favorite stories, it's a little kid or a very young person who does something spectacular. That's why I call this book: *Young Heroes of the Bible*.

Let's begin.

CHAPTER 1

WHAT TO DO WITH A VERY SHARP AX

The Story of Abraham as a Kid

YOU HAVE PROBABLY HEARD of Abraham. When Abraham was a little kid, he was called Abram. Later, when he became an adult and grew a beard, his name was changed to Abraham.

When I was a little kid, my name was Issur. Later, when I became an adult (and an actor), my name was changed to Kirk.

But this is the story of the little kid Abram. I am going to tell it just as I remember it from Sunday school, when I was eleven years old and my name was Issur.

So, we begin.

Little Abram lived four thousand years ago in a city called Ur, in a country called Babylonia, in a part of the world called Mesopotamia—which means "in the middle of rivers."

In my Sunday school we had a big map on the wall. It was the map of the Middle East. My teacher said that it's called the Middle East because it's the part of the world that's in the middle, between the three continents of Africa, Asia, and Europe. In the *middle* of the Middle East is a long and narrow strip of land between two big rivers called Tigris and Euphrates—"the rivers of Babylon"—and this strip of land was once called Mesopotamia. (It's now called Iraq; places change their names like people do.) And that's where Abram's city of Ur used to be.

Of course, the city of Ur isn't there anymore. It hasn't been there for a long time. And the great Mesopotamian civilization isn't there either. In fact, most of the great civilizations—the Babylonian, the Egyptian, the Persian, the Greek, the Roman—that were very powerful long ago don't exist now. For a time—say, about five hundred years—each civilization was very strong, very powerful, and everybody was afraid of it. But then something happened, and each one fell to pieces. Usually, another civilization came along that was stronger and more powerful, and its armies overran all the land in sight. Then that civilization was in power for a time until it too fell to pieces.

Why did that happen? Well, it had a lot to do with God.

Most of these civilizations worshiped idols—who were gods they made up. The Bible tells us that God created us; we can't create God. God is beyond and above us all. But these people *made* their gods—usually statues with weird heads—and then they convinced themselves that if they kept these idols happy, they would stay in power. Often, as time went on, their king—who was sometimes called emperor or pharaoh or caesar or czar—would decide he was god. When that happened, it was not long before the country fell to pieces.

But, I learned that later. When I was a kid in Sunday school, we pretty much stuck to learning about Ur, because it was Abram's hometown.

Ur was a beautiful place. It was really a big city. The streets were paved like our streets. Although back then they didn't have cement, they used clay, which—when dried in the hot sun—got very hard just like cement. They had apartment houses—two and three stories high—with pretty terraces that had flowers growing from flower boxes. They had a library, but it didn't have books in it like ours, because they didn't have paper. Instead, they wrote on triangular tablets made of clay, which—like their streets—were baked in the sun or in a fireplace until they got hard.

I'm sure that if I lived in Ur, I would get sick of clay after a while. Not only that, those books must have been pretty heavy to carry around. You had to be very strong.

When I was a kid, I complained about having to carry around all my books. But then I realized that it could be much worse. I could be living in Ur and carrying around these things that were as heavy as bricks! (Did that stop me from complaining? Only for a day.)

Of course, Abram was very strong. He went to school carrying his book bags, and he listened to his teachers. His school was a little different from our schools. For one thing, it was pretty messy. On his desk, Abram had a slab of mud. That's what clay looks like before it's baked. And he wrote on it with a stick. When he made a mistake, he could erase it very quickly before his teacher saw it. He just rubbed it over with the palm of his hand.

Abram was a good boy, and he studied hard. When you study hard, you learn a lot—and the more you learn, the more you want to know. So, Abram had a lot of questions. And it seems that the questions that bothered him the most were about God.

The people of Ur, like the people all over the country of Babylonia, worshiped many idols. The biggest idol that they worshiped was called Nergal. Today, we would call Nergal Satan. He was "the god of death and king of the underworld." Archaeologists digging in dirt in the Middle East have discovered baked clay pictures of Nergal carrying a sickle for cutting off people's heads. He kind of looked like a picture of the grim reaper from horror stories. (I was once the grim reaper on Halloween, and I carried a sickle made out of cardboard.)

The people of Ur had built a huge temple to Nergal in the middle of the city. The temple looked like a pyramid with steps on every side. It was called a ziggurat. At

the top of the ziggurat was a small room with a gold table where the people of Ur put gifts for Nergal.

They went to the temple often to bring sacrifices to Nergal so that he would be happy. But nobody knew if Nergal was happy, because he never spoke. So, everyone was afraid that if they made him unhappy—or, worse yet, angry—their city might be destroyed.

They did everything they could think of to keep him satisfied. They brought him delicious fruit and freshly baked bread. But in the morning the gifts were still lying there on the gold table, with flies buzzing all around. They killed cows and sheep and brought the slaughtered animals to the temple. But in the morning the carcasses were still there, rotting away. Of course, Nergal had eaten nothing. He was just an idol. Yet, the people never gave up trying. They brought him pretty maidens. They even brought him babies. Yes, they even killed tiny, defenseless babies, hoping to keep their god happy.

I mean—what was wrong with those people?

Well, the biggest thing that was wrong with them was that they were constantly afraid. They were afraid of things they didn't know. They thought the earth was flat and they were afraid of falling off the edge—they didn't know that the earth is round and we don't fall off it because of the pull of gravity. They thought the sun was a fiery monster—they didn't know that the sun is a star, ninety-three million miles away from the earth, which keeps the earth warm with its radiating energy. They thought the moon had superpowers—they didn't know that the moon is just a very large, pockmarked rock that shines only because its surface reflects the light of the sun. They thought the wind and the rain and anything they couldn't understand were gods. And they were afraid of them all. People will do pretty terrible things when they are afraid. A lot of evil in the world comes from fear.

Because they were so afraid, the people of Ur worshiped many idols. Besides the big boss, Nergal, they had lots of smaller gods. In fact, if you had a chance to visit a house in Ur, you would see it crowded with clay statues (yes, more clay) of all kinds of gods. They looked like dolls, but some had funny ears, others had big heads, and some had small heads and big feet or big hands.

At the entrance of every home there would be a little wooden box—that kind of looked like a doghouse—in which the "house god" lived. There would be a "fertility god" on a shelf in the bedroom—fertility gods would supposedly help their owners have more children. And on a shelf in the kitchen they might have a "rain god," so that plants would grow, and there would be fruit and vegetables to eat. In the backyard they might have a "sun god," so that the sun would shine and they could get a tan.

If you lived in Ur and you wanted a new god for your house, you had to go to the idol shop, and you better bring a big bag of coins.

Here comes a shock! Boy, was I surprised when I read about this!

The owner of the idol shop in Ur was none other than Mr. Terach—Abram's father.

Abram's dad's store was very big—it was like a supermarket. In fact, it was the biggest shop at the bazaar, which is what a mall was called in those days. Above the entrance there hung a big sign that said: WE HAVE A GOD FOR EVERY OCCASION.

So, you can understand why Abram would have a lot of questions about religion, and gods and idols.

He asked his father questions like: "How does the sun god make the sun shine?"

But his father only answered, "Keep quiet, Abram, and do your homework." (My father said the same thing to me, and it didn't feel good—not when you have an important question.)

So Abram asked his teacher at school, "What does Nergal do during the day?"

But his teacher only answered, "Keep quiet, Abram, or you will have to stay after school as punishment."

After a while Abram stopped asking questions and kept quiet. And he discovered that when he was very quiet, a small voice in his head whispered things to him.

The small voice told Abram that the adults of Ur did not know the answers to his questions. The small voice told Abram that he would have to figure out these things all by himself. The small voice told Abram that the place to start was his father's store.

So, one day, instead of going to school, Abram went to his father's store. In the back of the store was a building that was very mysterious. It had no windows, so no one could see inside, but on top, there was a chimney from which smoke billowed out. This building was always locked up, except when his father was working there. Abram didn't know what his father did inside, because he was never allowed in. When he had asked questions about it, he was told, as usual, to keep quiet. What went on inside there was known only to grown-ups, not children.

Abram was careful that no one would see him. He hid around the corner of the building, and from his hiding place, he watched his father's slave chopping wood right in front of the entrance.

Yes, his father had a slave, a person captured in war who had to work for free. It wasn't right to make people work and not pay them, but Ur was a bad place and everybody there did it.

The slave had an ax with a very shiny blade, and he swung it over his head and brought it down on large chunks of wood, chopping them up into smaller pieces so they would burn more easily.

Abram couldn't figure out how he would get past the slave and through the door. Then, the small voice whispered an idea to him.

When the slave stopped to wipe the sweat from his forehead, Abram picked up a pebble and threw it at a big palm tree growing on the other side of the entrance. The pebble thudded against the bark of the tree, bounced off, and fell near the slave. He looked up, puzzled. *Was the tree raining pebbles?* But then he just shrugged his shoulders, and went back to work.

Abram tried it again, and this time the pebble hit the man right in the head. The slave seemed annoyed, but not enough to interrupt his task. Then, Abram tried the same thing with a small coin.

Now, he had the slave's attention. The man picked up the coin and walked over to the tree to see if there was more money up there. Seeing none, he went around and behind the tree to investigate more closely.

This was the chance Abram had been hoping for. Quickly, he scurried from his hiding place and sneaked inside the building.

At first, he couldn't see a thing. But it was only for a little while, until his eyes got adjusted to the darkness inside.

Then he saw his father sitting at a table with his back to him. Abram held his breath, but his father didn't hear him come in; he was too busy.

Quickly, Abram ducked behind a cupboard and then carefully peeked out from behind it. *What was his father doing?*

It seemed to Abram that his father was playing with mud. He was kneading it like dough for bread.

This puzzled Abram very much. But he couldn't see too clearly. The only light came from a fire in a large brick fireplace at the far end of the room.

After a while his father stood up, and now Abram could see what Mr. Terach had been doing. His father had just made an idol out of clay. It looked like a large doll with big ears and big nose and big feet and big hands. In one big hand this idol held a big sickle. It looked like Nergal Junior.

Mr. Terach carried the figure to the fire and set it inside to bake.

While Nergal Junior was baking, Mr. Terach made another statue, much smaller and fatter—a fertility god—and put it in the oven too.

After what seemed like a long time to Abram, they were ready—two freshly baked gods. Mr. Terach took them out of the fire, being careful not to get burned. He set them aside to cool off, and a little while later, carried them both out of the building into the shop next door.

Abram couldn't believe it.

These gods didn't come from heaven. They came from his father's factory. Minutes before they had been nothing but mud.

Very disturbed, Abram sneaked out of the building and went home. How could these gods have any power? They were just lumps of lifeless clay!

That evening his father called him over after dinner.

Oh no, thought Abram, *did he find out I didn't go to school today?*

But his father only gave him a kindly smile. "Why are you so serious, Abram?" he asked.

"Oh, I was just thinking," Abram mumbled.

"Well, maybe you think too much. I see that you are studying very hard, perhaps you don't play enough."

"I play," Abram said, knowing that he was sounding kind of stupid.

But his father didn't seem to notice.

"I think you deserve a special treat," Mr. Terach continued. "Tomorrow, you won't have to go to school. Tomorrow, I will be away on business, and I am going to put you in charge of the store."

"What? Me?" Abram had terribly mixed feelings. This sure was a strange turn of events. As a reward for being such a good boy—which he knew he had not been, at least, not that day—he was being put in charge of his father's store, which, right now, seemed more like a punishment. How could he sit behind a counter selling gods when he knew they were worthless?

"Well, smile!" his father was saying. "It is an honor for someone as young as you to be given such a big responsibility."

Abram forced his lips to curl upward. He didn't say anything. In all that time of keeping quiet, he learned that sometimes silence is best.

The next day he sat behind the counter in his father's store, wishing and hoping no one would come in.

But wishing and hoping doesn't do it. Soon enough a man walked in.

"Where is Mr. Terach?" he asked.

"My father is away on business. Perhaps you'd like to come in tomorrow when he is here."

"No," said the man. "I need help now. I am getting old. I'm already fifty years old and I don't have any children. I need a fertility god right away."

"I'm sorry," said Abram. "But we are out of fertility gods just now."

"No, you're not," said the man. "There he is, right on the second shelf." And the man pointed to the fat idol that his father had made yesterday.

"You want that one?" Abram asked surprised.

"Yes, that one!" said the man, growing irritated with the boy, whom he assumed must be pretty stupid.

"But you are fifty years old," said Abram.

"Yes, that's right."

"That god is only a day old—how can he help you?"

The man looked at Abram strangely, then he turned around and left the store without saying another word.

Abram breathed a big sigh of relief. He was happy that the man didn't spend his money on the worthless idol. But the good feeling didn't last long, because very shortly another customer walked in.

It was a young woman, and she looked as if she had been crying.

"I need a house god, please, the biggest one you have." And she pulled out a bag of coins.

"Why do you want to buy a house god?" Abram asked.

"Because . . . because . . ." she stammered, and tears started flowing down her cheeks.

Abram offered her a chair since she looked as if she was going to collapse. She sat down in it heavily.

"Last night robbers came into our house, and . . . and . . . my husband tried to stop them and . . . they beat him up and . . ."

Her whole body was shaking with sobs now, and Abram didn't know what to do.

"The house god didn't protect him . . . and now I'm so afraid. . . . They ran away before they could steal anything, but I am so afraid that they might come back and hurt us again. So I brought all the money I have to buy a bigger god."

Abram knew he couldn't take this poor woman's money—all the money she had in the world.

"Listen," he said. "If the last god didn't protect you, who is to say that the next one will? Maybe it would be better if you bought a big lock with your money, or maybe . . . you know . . . I have a great idea!"

The woman looked at him through her tears.

"Get a big dog!"

"You know," said the woman, "for a little kid you are pretty smart."

She put her money away and left the store.

Abram felt very relieved. That had been a close call. He couldn't take that poor brokenhearted woman's money. He was glad he had come up with an idea that might really help her.

He was feeling happy about that, and then the small voice in his head whispered: "What if another customer comes in? What will you do?"

Thinking about it, Abram panicked. His ploys wouldn't work with everybody, he knew that. Maybe he should just close up the store. But tomorrow, when he wasn't there, his father would be selling these worthless lumps of clay to more unsuspecting people.

Suddenly, the small voice gave Abram another idea.

Quickly, he went out back to the woodpile. Against it leaned the ax that the slave had been using to chop wood. Abram touched the shiny blade—it was very sharp. It would do the job.

The ax was pretty heavy, but not so heavy that Abram couldn't carry it. He brought it into the store. Holding on to the handle with both hands, he raised the ax high into the air and brought the blade down smack in the middle of the head of the nearest idol. It shattered into many pieces. He raised the ax again, and again brought it down, smashing a second idol. It was easier than he thought. When he smashed the third one, he started to laugh. It felt good to smash the idols.

Abram continued. After a while he was covered with sweat from the effort, but he didn't mind. He knew he was doing the right thing. And that gave him great satisfaction.

Finally, all the idols were destroyed except one—the biggest one, Nergal Junior. Abram looked at the idol. It had a mean look on its clay face, and it wielded a sickle in its big fat hands. Abram smiled. He broke off the sickle and stuck the ax that he had been using to smash the statues in the big idol's hands.

Then he closed up the shop.

That night, when his father came home, he wanted to know how business had gone that day.

"I didn't sell anything," said Abram.

"Nothing?" Mr. Terach was surprised.

"No, not a one."

"Well, I guess people don't like doing business with a child," Mr. Terach reasoned. "Don't feel bad, Abram. You'll do better when you are a little older."

"I don't feel bad, Father," said Abram, and he meant it.

The next morning the principal called him out of class. "Your father wants to see you right away—you must go to his shop immediately."

Abram obeyed, bracing himself for the encounter.

When he got to the store, he found his father pacing among the broken clay statues so furious his whole face was red.

"What happened here yesterday?" he shouted.

"Oh, well . . . the idols got into a fight."

"What?"

"Yes, they all wanted my lunch, and the biggest one got the ax and started smashing the others."

"You are lying!" Mr. Terach could yell very loud when he was angry.

"No, I'm not! That's what happened. That big one did it!"

"Liar! That idol can't do anything. It can't even move. It's just a statue!"

"I know," said Abram quietly. "And you know. They are worthless statues. Yet you sell them to people who believe they are gods that can do things for them."

"Don't talk back to me—I am your father!"

"You cheat people."

Mr. Terach was incensed. He picked up a stick and hit Abram with it.

"Father, Father, please don't!" cried the little boy. But Terach was so angry, he had lost his senses. He hit the poor kid again and again. And when his anger was spent, he dropped the stick and left the store.

Poor Abram was huddled in the corner crying. He hurt all over. His father had been cheating people, and now he beat him up for saying so. He cried for a very long time, and then he picked himself up and walked out of the store.

He walked down the streets of Ur, but he was not going home. He was going as far away from home as he could get. Abram was leaving Ur.

He walked through a gate in the city wall, and immediately beautiful farmland opened up before him. Here canals brought the water from the Euphrates River to irrigate groves of fig and date trees and fields of corn and barley.

The slaves were hard at work in the fields and they

did not pay attention to the little boy who was slowly walking past them, his head hanging down mournfully.

The groves were pretty tall, so Abram could not see what was behind them, but when he got to their edge, he finally looked up to see a strange new world—the wilderness.

Before him stretched beautiful mountains covered with gnarled little shrubs and bright-colored wildflowers—pink and yellow and purple. Above him, the sky was a crystal blue, and birds danced and sang in the clear air.

How different it was from all the clay-paved streets and clay-built structures of the busy city. How peaceful.

As Abram walked on, he surprised a herd of gazelles, which had been grazing peacefully on some shrubs. They took off into the wilderness, jumping over rocks as lightly as fairies.

He marveled how everything got here—the flowers, the birds, the gazelles. This wilderness was not land tilled by slaves or fed by irrigation canals. It just existed, dependent on nobody. *Not nobody,* thought Abram. *It was dependent upon a god, but who was this god?*

For sure he knew it wasn't Nergal. How could "the king of death" be responsible for all this *life*. Perhaps the earth was god, since nothing would exist if the earth didn't feed it. But then the earth by itself cannot make things grow; it needs rain. Perhaps the rain was god, but the rain must leave the sky when the sun shines. So the sun must be god. He knelt down on the ground and bowed to the sun, saying a long prayer with his eyes closed. It was such a long prayer that when he looked up again, the sky was dark. The sun had set, and now the moon was rising. If the moon could make the sun move over, then the moon must rule over the sun, so perhaps the moon is god.

Abram was very tired from thinking so much, and still he had not figured out who god was.

And then he heard that little voice inside his head whispering again. The little voice said: "You cannot *see* God, because everything you see was made by God."

Yes, of course! God was the Creator. God had made everything! God was above everything and inside everything! That's why you can't see God!

And Abram realized that the little voice that had been giving him such good advice all along was the voice of God inside him. He now knew this was the truth.

There were not many little gods—some good and

some bad—there was only one God who was all good.

That is where the name God came from. It is the word "good" with an *o* left out.

And that is why we believe—all the Jews, Christians, and Muslims, almost three billion people all over the world—in one God.

Little Abram figured it out for us, when he was just a kid.

And that's why he is my hero!

CHAPTER 2

EVEN A CAMEL GETS THIRSTY SOMETIMES

The Story of Rebecca as a Young Girl

WHEN I WAS A KID, I had six sisters. Three were older and three younger. That put me right in the middle. My father wasn't home much, so I was left mostly with my mother and my sisters. Me, the only boy. I went around saying that I hated girls and that I wanted a brother.

But when I grew up, I realized that I had been very unfair to my sisters. It was not their fault that I didn't have a brother. And despite the fact that I told them I hated girls, they were very nice to me. They played ball with me, like a brother would, but they also baked cookies for me, like a brother wouldn't.

One day—it was my twelfth birthday—my sisters surprised me with a special party. They all took turns giving me twelve slaps on my back until they just about knocked me over. But the delicious birthday cake they baked made up for it.

I have to admit that I loved my sisters. They were girls, but they were great.

This story is about another great girl—a real hero— by the name of Rebecca.

But before I tell you about Rebecca, I have to tell you first what happened to Abram, because it's important to the story.

Abram was a terrific kid. And when he grew up he was a pretty terrific adult too. That's when God changed his name. God added a letter, *h*, from God's own name—it is a secret name that we are not allowed to pronounce. God put that letter *h* right into the middle of Abram's name and Abram became Abra-h-am.

Abraham continued to listen to the little voice inside of him, and it told him to stay away from cities like Ur. So Abraham went to live in the wilderness. He had herds of sheep and goats and camels, and he was constantly on the move, looking for the best pastures for his animals. He lived in a tent made out of animal hides, and he wrote on scrolls also made out of animal hides, and even his water jar was a bag made out of animal hides. (You can see that Abraham was pretty sick of clay, which also would have been very heavy to carry around if you walked as far as he did.)

Even though I really didn't like old men with long beards, I made an exception for Abraham, because he was so nice. The Bible says Abraham was full of *chesed,* which means "loving kindness." He was kind to everybody, especially little kids, and you can be sure he never beat any of them with a stick like his father did.

Since he was always on the move, Abraham was meeting all sorts of people and inviting them to dinner. His wife, Sarah, loved people just as much as Abraham, and she would make their guests feel very welcome. She really knew the meaning of hospitality—which is being very nice to strangers. She was also a really great cook, and she made delicious bread and many delicacies for dinner. While they were eating, Abraham would tell his guests what he knew about God. To everyone he met, this made sense, and very soon, a whole lot of people had joined him.

This is how Abraham got to be so famous. As an adult, Abraham had many adventures with God, which are recorded in the Bible. But I won't tell them here; this book is just about kids.

Abraham had a son named Isaac. Someday, it would be his job to travel and invite people to dinner and to tell them about God. Someday, Isaac would inherit Abraham's mission. So it was very important that Isaac marry a very special girl. I say "girl" because in those days people got married very young. A girl who was fourteen would be considered old enough to marry.

Abraham thought and thought about where to find the best wife for Isaac. And then his wife, Sarah, died, and he was very, very sad. He knew she was the best wife that a man could ever have. Sarah, who was Isaac's mother of course, had come from Babylonia, just like Abraham had. And now, Abraham decided that he would start his search in her hometown.

For this task he appointed his trusted employee, an old fellow named Eliezer. (I can't get away from these old guys no matter how I try.) Abraham told Eliezer to go to a place between the two big rivers called Aram Naharayim, which means "Aram-of-Two-Rivers." (I don't know why they had such long names back then, but I will call it Rivercity because it's easier that way.)

Abraham made Eliezer promise to look very hard for a girl just like his wonderful, kind Sarah, who would have the gift of hospitality and would be nice to strangers.

Abraham knew that such a girl was a rare treasure

and probably very valuable to her family. He also knew that a good family might not want to let a city girl live in the wilderness, in tents tending animals, no less. So Abraham gave Eliezer many expensive presents to take with him to show that she would have lots of nice things in her new home and that she would be treated very well. There were so many presents that Eliezer needed ten camels just to load them all up.

Eliezer started out, and as he traveled toward Rivercity, he met other people on the road. When he asked directions to make sure he didn't get lost, everyone would tell him: "Don't go there, it's an awful place!" Or "Stay away from there, it's a city full of thieves and liars!" Or "All the people in Rivercity are criminals!"

Now Eliezer was getting worried. What would happen to him in Rivercity? But his employer, the good and wise Abraham, made him promise to go there and search for Isaac's wife, so he had to do it. Eliezer would never break his promise. And besides that, he trusted Abraham. If Abraham said, "Go to Rivercity," to Rivercity he must go!

He asked another person he met if the women of Rivercity were just as bad as the men, and he explained what kind of woman he was looking for. The traveler just shook his head. "All the men of this town are rogues," he said. "A good woman who came from among them would be like a lily among the thorns."

We had lots of thorn bushes around our house and I can tell you there was nothing pretty or nice about them. If my ball would land there, I would get all scratched up trying to retrieve it, and sometimes even would have to put on a Band-Aid. A lily is very different—it is delicate and white and it has a soft stem; my mother said a lily is hard to grow. Eliezer knew that too, and he was feeling pretty low by the time he arrived near Rivercity.

He decided not to go into town right away. He wasn't looking forward to this at all. Already, he'd met a few people from the town as he got near, and they yelled at him to get his camels out of the way. A big caravan of a rich man passed by, and they just about pushed him off the road. So Eliezer decided he wouldn't look for a rich girl for Isaac. She should be a girl who was already used to hard work, a girl who liked animals (because Abraham and Isaac had many sheep and goats and camels), and a girl who wasn't too proud and who didn't need to have servants and maids do the work for her.

For this reason, he made his camp by the city's well, where all the poor women would come to get water for cooking and washing.

Back then, big cities, even fancy ones like Ur and Rivercity, didn't have indoor plumbing. Pipes hadn't been invented yet. They had bathtubs, but they brought water in buckets from the wells that could be found in the center of town and also at the edge of town. So Eliezer told his camels to sit down near the well. When camels sit they actually kneel down—kneeling is sitting to a camel.

And Eliezer waited. Lots of girls came to the well, and when he asked them who they were, they all said they were slave girls working for rich people.

And then he saw a girl coming, and right away he knew she was an unusual girl.

She was dressed in a very pretty cloak—a kind of

poncho with no sleeves and a hole cut out for the head. Hers was very cheerful, with stripes of many colors. This was not the drab brown robe of a slave; this girl was somebody. Even in the distance, Eliezer could see that she waved and said hello to everyone that she met. Even though she was dressed in nice clothes, she was not too proud to wish the slave girls a nice day.

When she came closer, Eliezer saw that she was very pretty. She had a sweet smiling face and long black curly hair that was tied back with a narrow white ribbon around her forehead. She was carrying a clay jar for her water. (They had a lot of clay things in Rivercity, just like they did in Ur.)

Maybe she is the one, Eliezer thought hopefully, and he said a prayer that God should give him a sign. It was a quick prayer, because he didn't have time for a long one. The girl was coming his way and smiling.

"Hello," she said. "You look like you traveled far."

"Yes," said Eliezer. "Yes, I have."

"Welcome to Rivercity," she said.

"Thank you." Eliezer bowed his head, but did not get up.

"Oh," she said, "you must be very tired. Can I help you in any way?"

What an unusual girl, thought Eliezer, and he answered, "I could use a drink of water."

Now if Eliezer had asked me for a drink of water I would have said, "You're sitting next to a well, dummy. Get up and get a drink."

But Rebecca did no such thing. She immediately ran to the well as fast as she could, dipped her jar in, and then ran to him with the water.

Eliezer drank from her jar and thanked her, thinking all the while, *This is a very hospitable girl.*

"What is your name?" he asked, introducing himself.

"My name is Rebecca."

What a pretty name, thought Eliezer.

And then Rebecca did the most unusual thing. She ran back to the well and filled her jar, and ran back again. "Oh no," Eliezer said, "I've had plenty to drink. I'm not thirsty anymore."

"But your camels," she said, "your camels must be very thirsty."

The camels *were* very thirsty. She gave the water to the first one and he gulped it all down.

"He is a big camel, he probably needs more." She ran back again. And again the camel gulped all the water. She ran back again and again and again. The camel drank fourteen jars of water! To a camel a gallon of water is a like a glassful is to us.

But there were ten camels. And they were all very thirsty, because they had been traveling a long way.

Camels are very interesting animals. I rode a camel once on my trip to Israel. I'll never forget it. The camel has big feet soft as pillows, and he puts them down very carefully, so you sit there rocking back and forth and it's very pleasant.

Some camels have two humps and some have one. I don't know if Eliezer's camels had one hump or two, because the Bible doesn't tell us this. I used to think they stored their water in that big hump, but I was wrong. That hump is made of fat, and when they are hungry they can use that fat to supply energy for their travels. But camels do drink a lot of water—as much as twenty-two gallons at a time—that goes to every part of their body. They use this water sparingly; that's why they can travel over the desert for many days without a drink. So you can imagine how much work it was for Rebecca to water all those animals!

When we read this story in Sunday school, I said out loud, "Boy was that Rebecca dumb! What did she carry all that water for?" My teacher got mad at me and as punishment I had to write a hundred times: "Rebecca was not dumb—she was kind. It is never dumb to be kind." Believe me, I learned my lesson.

Okay, so Rebecca was a very kind girl, and she demonstrated to Eliezer that she had the perfect qualities to be a good wife to Isaac, just the kind of wife Abraham wanted for his son.

As she was running with the water, beads of sweat stood out on her forehead and her pretty hair ribbon fell off, so her hair was flying. Eliezer just shook his head in wonderment. Never once did she even look at Eliezer to help her. She could have easily said: "What are you standing there for and just looking at me? Don't you see your camels are thirsty? Grab a jar and get some water too!" She could have said that, but she didn't say it, and the Bible tells us that she didn't even *think* it. She didn't know why Eliezer let her do all the work—maybe he was handicapped, like he had only one leg or a bad back. If she asked him why he wasn't helping, he might have to explain his handicap and be embarrassed. Not embarrassing people is very important. It is a commandment in the Bible: "Never embarrass another person!"

This is the perfect girl for Isaac, I am sure, Eliezer thought.

When she finished, he bowed to her deeply and said, "Thank you so much. Because you have been so kind, I would like to give you a present."

"Oh no," said Rebecca, "I couldn't possibly accept a present. This was just a favor I did."

"This present is not from me, but from my master, Abraham. He asked me to give it when I found a very special girl who might be the wife to his son, Isaac."

Rebecca looked at him surprised and she blushed.

"Please, please, accept it. My master, Abraham, is very rich and this is just a small token."

And he handed her a beautiful wooden box. She opened it and inside were two thick gold bracelets and a nose ring. "Oh, they are beautiful!" she said, and put them on right away. (I have learned in life that all girls like jewelry. My sisters did, and every girl and woman I have ever known liked rings and bracelets . . . and necklaces and earrings too. Of course, I haven't known any girls who liked nose rings, though some people do. I wonder if it gets in the way when you get a cold and have to blow your nose.)

Rebecca thanked Eliezer very much for the bracelets and the nose ring. Then Eliezer said, "I am looking for a place to stay for the night—for me and my camels."

"Come with me," said Rebecca. "We have a large house, and I will find you a room and a stable with straw for your camels."

So they started walking to her house, and Eliezer saw that something was bothering Rebecca. She seemed to get more and more nervous as they walked through the clay-paved streets of the city and got closer and closer to her house.

What is bothering her? wondered Eliezer, and he asked her about her family.

"My mother died some years ago," said Rebecca, "but my father is alive. His name is Betuel, and he is the son of Milkah and Nahor."

"Milkah and Nahor?" exclaimed Eliezer. He could

hardly believe his ears. Milkah, Rebecca's grandmother, had been Sarah's sister. And Nahor, Rebecca's grandfather, had been Abraham's brother. Rebecca was a relative! This was great. No wonder she showed qualities of kindness and hospitality just like Abraham and Sarah. Now, Eliezer was sure that she was the right wife for Isaac. He said a silent prayer of thanks to God for helping him find this girl.

Thanking God is a very good thing to do—when things go my way I always remember to thank God. When I was a kid I didn't do it, but I was wrong. We should never take good things for granted, we should always thank God or the person who makes good things possible in our lives.

Eliezer continued to ask questions about her family and found out that Rebecca had a brother named Laban. He noticed that she seemed uncomfortable talking about her father and her brother.

"Are they good people?" he asked, following his suspicions.

She did not answer, but hung her head down in shame. *Ahh,* thought Eliezer, *I better remember the warnings I've heard on the road. This is a town of thieves and liars. I better be careful.*

When they came to the house—which was large

and made of clay with many courtyards and stables for animals—Rebecca's brother Laban came out. He saw Eliezer and his caravan of camels all loaded with goods, and he saw the gold bracelets shining in the sun on Rebecca's arm. Laban was a thief and he immediately began to plot how to steal some of Eliezer's treasure. Meanwhile, he pretended to be gracious, and called out, "Oh, kind stranger! Come stay with us. Welcome, welcome!"

Eliezer bowed to him in greeting and immediately began to unload the sacks from his camels. He knew they were tired and hungry.

"Oh no," said Laban. "Leave that for later. Come, have something to eat."

"I can't, I must take care of my camels."

Eliezer knew that it is a commandment from God that you must immediately unload the animals' burden when you reach your destination. And, when your animals are hungry, you have to feed them first. Only then can you eat. That's what the Bible says.

So Eliezer took care of his camels, and then he went inside to meet Betuel, Rebecca's father, to ask him for his daughter's hand in marriage on behalf of Isaac.

Eliezer took one look at Betuel, who had a mean scowl on his face, and he didn't like him at all. Rebecca was clearly afraid of her father.

"Go and fix something to eat," Betuel barked at her, and shoved her in the direction of the kitchen. What a big difference from the way Abraham treated Sarah—always speaking softly to her with great respect and saying "please" and "thank you." *Poor girl,* thought Eliezer, *how did she grow up to be so good with such a nasty father and a no-good brother.*

Eliezer decided to waste no time. He quickly explained who he was and why he came there, and he gave them many presents—vintage wines, delicious honey, rare oils, precious blue stones called lapis lazuli, and beautiful robes dyed purple, a color that was very unusual and highly prized in those days. He explained that Abraham was very rich and that Isaac his son would be too, and that Rebecca would have everything she might want in her new home. He wanted to add: "Not to mention, that she'll be treated with respect like she isn't here." But he didn't say it, because he didn't want to cause her any trouble.

Betuel marveled at all the beautiful things. But he kept looking at the two bags that Eliezer hadn't opened. He was very curious about what was in them. He was greedy and he always wanted more than he got.

Finally, Eliezer finished presenting all the gifts, but the two bags remained unopened. Betuel scowled. He said, "Well, this is very nice, but Rebecca has the right to decide for herself whom she wants to marry. We have to ask her first."

"Of course, of course," said Eliezer. He waited while Betuel went into the kitchen to get Rebecca.

Betuel had a very gruff voice and even when he talked in a low tone, you could hear him. Eliezer wasn't eavesdropping, but he heard everything Betuel said in the kitchen.

"Rebecca, go out there and tell this man you want many more presents before you will consent to be the wife of Isaac."

"Oh no, Father, he's already given me a lot. And he

gave you a lot. I can't ask him for more."

"You will ask him because I tell you to," barked Betuel.

"I can't, Father. Please don't make me."

And then Eliezer heard a slap and Rebecca's cry of pain.

"You will do it or you will get a beating!" shouted Betuel.

He came out of the kitchen and addressed Eliezer, "My daughter is thinking it over." And then a crooked smile appeared on his face. "While we wait for her decision, let's have a big feast in honor of your visit."

Eliezer sighed. He wanted to get out of there as quickly as possible and save that sweet decent girl from these horrible people.

Very shortly, Rebecca came out of the kitchen with fresh pita bread and a big pot of delicious-smelling vegetable soup.

"Here, let me serve you myself!" Betuel jumped up, pretending to be gracious and grabbing the soup. He set the pot on the sideboard, next to a stack of bowls, and made a big show of stirring it with the ladle. Then he tasted it. "Oh, Rebecca, you didn't make it spicy enough."

"But, Father, I made it the way you like it."

"No, no, it needs more salt." He reached into a jar sitting on the top shelf. His big belly was blocking the way and Eliezer couldn't see that he sprinkled something into only one bowl. But it wasn't salt at all. It was poison.

Betuel put poison in Eliezer's bowl because he wanted Eliezer to die, so he could steal what was in the unopened bags.

Betuel almost succeeded. Eliezer didn't see that Betuel poisoned his soup. But God saw.

God is always watching over his people, and He immediately sent an angel to make sure that Eliezer didn't eat the poisoned soup.

Now, angels are invisible. We can't see them. I never saw one, but I have seen pictures of them in books.

It was a difficult assignment for this angel. He never

handled a situation like this before. How could he take away the poisoned bowl of soup from Eliezer? He was invisible, but the soup was not. It couldn't just float out of the room on a cloud. So the invisible angel squeezed himself onto the bench between Eliezer and Betuel—he was a skinny angel so he didn't take up much room. At first he planned to spill the soup, but then Betuel stood up. "Let's make a toast," he cried.

"Yes, a toast to our guest!" echoed Laban, standing also.

Eliezer smiled weakly as they gulped the wine.

That's when the angel got a better idea. His angel wings moved very fast, and he switched the bowls while they weren't looking.

Now Betuel had the bowl with the poison in it. But he didn't know it. And he ate it. The skinny angel giggled, but nobody could hear him.

Later, I think he got in trouble with God. He was supposed to protect Eliezer and not kill other people. He could have thrown the poisoned soup out. He wasn't supposed to improvise. That night, Betuel went to bed, and he never got up again. The poison killed him.

Laban, who was in on the plot, got scared. Eliezer was the one who was supposed to be dead, but instead, Eliezer woke up, said, "Good Morning," and went to feed his camels.

All this made Laban very uncomfortable. He said to Rebecca, "I don't want to have anything more to do with him. He is bad news. Let's just tell him to get out of here."

"I am going with him," said Rebecca.

"I forbid it."

"I don't care, I am going with him. He is a good man and his master, Abraham, is a man who walks with God. I want to be with people like them, not people like you. Don't even try to stop me."

And Laban didn't. Rebecca, even though she was only a girl of fourteen, was a strong person. Her goodness gave her strength. Whereas Laban's immorality made him weak.

Rebecca was a real hero, because it is very hard to be good when other people around you are bad.

When I was a kid, one day someone in the class brought in a pack of cigarettes and everybody tried smoking. Only one boy said that he wouldn't, because it was a bad thing to do. And everyone made fun of him for being a sissy. But he was right. Smoking is bad. He was a lone hero.

Rebecca was an even bigger hero, because she lived

in a whole city of liars and thieves. Nobody ever praised her for being a good girl, but she was good just the same.

She would make the perfect wife for Isaac, who soon would take over his father's mission of teaching people about the one God who is good.

Rebecca was happy to leave Rivercity. Gracefully, she climbed on top of one of Eliezer's camels and they started off together for the land of Canaan—that's where Israel is today and that's where Abraham and Isaac lived.

Meanwhile, Isaac had been waiting anxiously for Eliezer to return. Who would this girl be? What if Eliezer brought back someone he didn't like? Of course, he wouldn't have to marry her, but then Eliezer would have to make another long trip to find another girl.

Because he was anxious, Isaac went out into the open field to say a prayer for Eliezer's safe return.

As he was praying, he gradually became aware that something unusual was going on all around him. After he finished praying, he looked more closely.

All the rabbits were poking their heads out of their warrens. Deer were peeking out of the woods, standing perfectly still, their ears perked, staring into the distance. And then the birds started tweeting and flying excitedly about. Someone that the animals loved was coming. Then over the hill, a camel caravan appeared.

Isaac recognized Eliezer on the lead camel and behind him . . . yes, there was a girl, a girl the animals loved, a beautiful girl—Rebecca. She jumped off the camel and approached him. She had such a sweet friendly smile on her face. Isaac knew that she was the wife for him.

And they got married and lived happily ever after.

CHAPTER 3

A Spoiled Brat Who Grew Up To Be a Hero

The Story of Joseph as a Kid and a Young Man

REBECCA AND ISAAC had two sons—twins—Jacob and Esau. And then Jacob got married and he had twelve sons and one daughter.

This story is about one of Jacob's sons, Joseph.

Jacob, like his grandfather, Abraham, and his father, Isaac, believed in one God and made it his mission to teach this important truth to all the people that he would meet. But, unlike his ancestors who traveled all over with their sheep and goats and lived in tents, Jacob decided to try city life. After all, there were a lot of people living in the city, and he could have constant guests to dinner. In the wilderness, you had to sit and wait until the next caravan came, but in the city, all you had to do was just go around the corner and you would find another stranger.

The city he chose to live in was named Hebron. He picked Hebron—located in the southern part of the land of Canaan—because this is where his grandfather, Abraham, bought a cave to bury his grandmother, Sarah. In the old days when people died, they were buried in caves. This particular cave became very important to Jacob's family. His father, Isaac, and his mother, Rebecca, were buried in it. And he knew that someday he too would be buried in it. That cave is still there today—it is called the Cave of the Patriarchs—and you can visit it, but you are not allowed to go inside.

The one big problem with Hebron was that it was situated in a dry area. (No rivers here.) There was not much grass nearby for Jacob's many sheep and cattle and camels to eat, and no ponds for them to drink from. This meant that he had to send his animals far away to pasture, but he had his twelve sons to take turns looking after everything. The older ones did just that, but of course, the younger ones were still in school.

Of all Jacob's twelve sons, Joseph was his favorite. That's because from the time Joseph was very little, he was the best at everything he tried. He was very smart and he always learned everything quickly. He got A's on his tests in school. He won prizes for best scholarship and best penmanship and best this and best that. He always raised his hand first whenever the teacher asked a question.

When I was growing up, there was a kid like that in my school, and I hated his guts. I never had the chance to get anything right, because he was always first, the best, the greatest.

Joseph's brothers felt the same way. "Why does he always have to do everything right?" they grumbled. "Look at him. Teacher's pet . . . la-dee-da . . . la-dee-da."

Because Joseph was so good at everything, his father, Jacob, was very proud of him. And he praised him constantly. This, of course, irritated his brothers all the more, and they refused to play with him.

This made Joseph feel very sad and lonely.

Jacob tried to get the brothers to play with Joseph, and they promised they would, but when their father wasn't looking they just stuck their tongues out at the poor kid.

Jacob thought it wasn't fair that Joseph should be punished by the other kids for being good, so he decided to reward him with a special present. He went out and bought him a really terrific jacket. It was made out of the same kind of shiny material that Superman's and Batman's capes are made out of, and it was very colorful. The Bible calls it "a coat of many colors."

Joseph thought it was great! Wow, a special superhero outfit!

This was too much for the brothers. They hated him even more now for being the best and for having that great coat.

Now, being the best gradually went to Joseph's head. He started to think that just because he could do so many things so well, that he was better than everybody else.

This was a bad mistake.

Why? I learned in Sunday school that God gives us all special gifts. Some people are really good at playing the piano—and of course they get better if they practice. And some people are good at math—and they get better if they work out a lot of difficult problems. And some people are good at sports—and the more they play, the faster and stronger they become. But the original gift comes from God. So you can't take all the credit yourself. And you have to remember that other people have special gifts too. You are *not* better than everybody else.

Well, Joseph forgot that. He started to think that he was *too* good.

With that kind of attitude, he began to look for faults in other people. After a while he could only see the mistakes they made. But sometimes he was wrong.

One day, when he came home from school, his father gave him a big basket full of food. "Your brothers are watching after the sheep outside of town. They won't be able to come home tonight for dinner. Go and take them this food."

"I'll do my best," said Joseph. (This was his favorite thing to say, because it reminded people that he was the best.)

He hurried out of town, but before he was even halfway to where his brothers were, he saw a lamb that had been killed by a wolf. He turned right around and ran home to his father. "Daddy, Daddy!" he yelled so loud, the neighbors could hear him.

"What happened?" asked Jacob.

"They are not doing their job!"

"Who isn't?"

"Reuben and Judah and Simon and Dan . . . they are not doing what you told them to do."

"Your brothers are not watching the sheep?"

"No. I saw a lamb that was killed by wolves. They weren't watching and the wolves attacked the sheep."

Jacob became very upset. He went with Joseph to see what was going on. When they got to the dead lamb, Jacob bent over and checked its ear for a special mark. Jacob would paint a *J* in the ear, so that he would know which sheep belonged to him in case one got lost.

But there was no *J* in the ear. There was an *L*. This lamb belonged to a neighbor named Lev. It must have run away from Lev's flock, got lost, and was killed by a wolf.

"This isn't our lamb, Joseph. You were wrong to accuse your brothers."

"Well . . . I thought . . ."

"I know what you thought. But you shouldn't jump to conclusions and accuse people. Remember that."

But Joseph forgot.

Another time he heard his brother Judah say something to his brother Reuben. It sounded like "The boy is lazy."

He ran to Jacob again. "Daddy, Daddy, Judah told Reuben that I am lazy."

Jacob called them over. "Are you saying bad things about your brother?" he demanded.

"What?" said Judah.

"Did you call him lazy?"

"No, I didn't. He is many things I don't like, but he isn't lazy."

"That's right, Dad," said Reuben. "He didn't say anything about Joseph being lazy."

"I heard it!" yelled Joseph. "I heard it. Judah said: 'The boy is lazy!'"

Reuben started to laugh. "No, he said, 'The sky is hazy.' We were talking about the weather."

Judah was not laughing. "Stop being such a tattle-tale," he hissed.

"Apologize to your brothers," Jacob commanded.

"I'm sorry," said Joseph. But he didn't mean it, and his brothers knew it.

"He deserves a good spanking," said Judah. "And if father doesn't give it to him, I will."

Of course, Jacob wouldn't punish Joseph, which was a big mistake in my opinion. Jacob didn't see that Joseph was becoming a spoiled brat.

Once, when I was a kid, an older boy stole my lunch. He wouldn't give it back. He ate half of it. I tried to get the rest back, but he wouldn't let me have it. He was bigger than me, and he kicked me and threw the rest of my food in the garbage. I was hungry and very upset. I went to his house and told his mother what happened.

His mother called him over. "Ricky (that was his name), did you steal this boy's lunch?"

"No, Mama. I never touched it. I never even saw it."

"You're a liar—" I started to say, but his mother cut me off.

"You terrible boy—making up stories about Ricky. You go home right now."

What could I do? I went home hungry. His mother was very unfair, and she should have punished him.

So, I understand perfectly well how Judah felt about Joseph not ever being punished by his father. And because of that things got worse.

The Bible tells us that another of Joseph's special gifts was dreaming. He could go to sleep and in his dreams see pictures of things that were going to happen. Often these pictures were symbolic—that is, they stood for something else—but Joseph's gift allowed him to figure out what the symbols meant.

One night he had a special dream and he bragged about it to his brothers. This is how we read it in Sunday school straight from the Bible: "Joseph said to them: 'Hear this dream which I have dreamt. We were binding sheaves in the field when suddenly my sheaf stood up and remained upright. Then your sheaves gathered around and bowed low to my sheaf.'"

Then he explained to them what these symbols meant. Sheaves, which are clumps of wheat stalks, represented the brothers in the dream. The dream predicted that someday the brothers, just like the sheaves, would have to bow to Joseph who would become a very important man.

The brothers didn't like hearing this at all. It was insulting, and they hated him even more.

I don't blame them. I mean, Joseph couldn't help having the dream, but he should have kept it to himself. He should have known that his brothers were going to be upset. But being quiet was not easy for Joseph.

Then he had another dream. And, of course, he had

to tell this one to his brothers too. Here's how the Bible says he told it: "Behold!" (That's how they talked in those days.) "I dreamt another dream. The sun, the moon and eleven stars were bowing to me." And of course, right away, he explained that the sun was his father, and the moon his mother, and the eleven stars were his brothers.

This one was too much even for his father. And for the first time Jacob scolded Joseph right in front of his brothers. But it was too late—the brothers were now so angry that they couldn't see straight.

They went off to watch the sheep, grumbling and saying mean things under their breath.

Joseph didn't go; he was still too young for this responsible job. His father's flocks were very large and it took much organization to make sure they were all herded to the right places, where they could eat good grass and have water to drink.

A few days later, as Joseph was sitting in the window and looking up at the sky, he heard the voice of his father. "Joseph, please go check on your brothers. They have been working with the sheep for days, and I want to know if they are all right."

"I'll do my best, Dad," Joseph chirped in his usual way.

He picked up the basket of food that his father had prepared for his brothers and went on his way. They were very far, and it took him a long time to find them.

Meanwhile, the brothers were busy rounding up the animals, and they were all sweaty. They hadn't had a bath since they left home and being dirty made them extra grumpy. Their mood didn't improve when they saw Joseph coming toward them in the distance, skipping along, swinging the food basket, and whistling a tune. He looked clean and spiffy in his freshly laundered superhero outfit.

They stared at him with hatred.

Dan said, "Here comes the dreamer. You know, I could just kill him."

"That would teach him a lesson," said Reuben, laughing at his own joke.

"No, I mean it. I've had enough of him."

"Yes," said Simon. "I say we kill him."

"He deserves it," chimed in Judah.

"You can't mean it!" Reuben was shocked to think they might be serious. "What would we tell Father?"

"We'd say that a wolf ate him."

They all laughed in agreement. "Yeah, then we'll see what happens with his dream," said Simon.

Reuben was alarmed. They did mean it! They really

wanted to kill Joseph! He saw how angry they were and he realized that he wouldn't be able to talk them out of it. So he said, "You know what? We don't want his blood on our hands. I have a better idea. There is a pit over there that was once a well. Let's just throw him in it and leave him. No one will find him and he'll die eventually. But we won't be the ones who killed him." Reuben thought that if they threw Joseph in the pit and left him there, he could come back later and rescue him.

"The pit is a great idea," said Simon.

"The snakes will bite him and he'll die," said Dan, seconding the plan.

Little did they know that there were no poisonous snakes in the pit. I'd like to think that the skinny angel who had saved Eliezer was doing his job again and had scared the snakes away. For sure, God would have given him another chance. Or maybe angels just get one job apiece and then they retire. I don't know because I never saw any angels to ask them how it works in heaven.

By now, Joseph had come close. He waved his arms. "Hi, hi! I brought you food. You must be hungry. Good thing I did my best to get here quickly."

Oh, how the brothers hated that word—"best." To

them it was a fighting word, and they were ready to fight.

Menacingly, they stood up and circled him, as he stared at them with bewilderment, unable to guess what they were up to. Perhaps they were playing some sort of game.

"Now!" yelled Dan, and Judah, Simon, and Levi pounced on Joseph. They held him down and the others joined in to rip off his beautiful coat.

"What are you doing?" Joseph screamed. But they didn't answer him as they dragged him, kicking, screaming, and struggling to the pit.

They threw him in and shook hands with each other, laughing. Down deep from the pit, Joseph could be heard crying, "Why? Why?"

Dan bent over the edge. "Because you are a tattletale!"

"Because you think you are better than all of us," shouted Levi.

"Let's see if the snakes think you are the best," said Simon, laughing.

"You'll be the *best* dinner they ever ate," added Judah.

Reuben, who had participated in none of this, stood by saying nothing. It revolted him when he heard Dan say, "And speaking of dinner—let's eat." Here, their younger brother was crying in anguish and they weren't bothered in the least. It wasn't going to spoil their appetite. He went away in disgust. *When they fall asleep, I'll rescue Joseph,* he thought.

Meanwhile, the brothers had ripped apart the basket

of food that Joseph brought and they began to gorge themselves on the delicious food.

Having finished eating, Judah stood up to stretch. Joseph's cries had turned to pitiful whimpers. "Stop whining," Judah shouted, "or I'll—" Suddenly he stopped, distracted by a sight emerging in the distance.

It was a caravan, a very large caravan with many, many camels transporting goods from Mesopotamia to Egypt. (The land of Canaan lay right in between the two empires and for that reason was a very important thoroughfare.)

The brothers had seen such large caravans before. They knew that they carried the things that Egypt treasured and needed—spices and slaves.

When I read about this in Sunday school, I thought that it meant Egyptians liked Mexican food and the spices were chili peppers and tabasco and paprika. (I used to like spicy food a lot, but nowadays I get an upset stomach when I eat it.) My teacher explained,

though, that the Egyptians had never heard of Mexico because nobody had yet sailed across the Atlantic Ocean to America, and that the Egyptians liked different spices—like balm and balsam. Balm is an oil that smells minty, and balsam is a syrup that comes from camphor trees and smells like turpentine. I don't know why the Egyptians were so crazy about something that smells like turpentine—ugh!—but my teacher said that maybe they used these spices for medicine.

The other thing that Egyptians valued were slaves. They would buy people as if they were cows or donkeys and make them work hard without paying anything. It's a good thing we don't do that today in the civilized world!

When Judah noticed the caravan, he got an idea.

"Hey, look," he called out to his other brothers who were still eating.

"So? It's a caravan," said Dan, a piece of meat hanging from his mouth.

"Don't you get it?" Judah was excited. "This is a solution to our problem. This is the way to get rid of Joseph. We can sell him to those slave traders."

"Good idea," said Dan, seeing the practical aspects right away. "We'll be rid of the pest and we'll make some money too."

"Quick," said Simon, "let's get him out of the pit before the caravan passes by."

They took a rope that they used to tie up the goats and threw it down the pit. Joseph grabbed it and they pulled him out. "Oh, thank you, thank you." He was so happy to be freed from his prison. "You really scared me—that wasn't a funny joke."

"It's not over yet," Simon sneered maliciously.

"Yeah." Dan laughed. "We're giving you a special present—a one-way ticket to Egypt."

"What?" Joseph was aghast. And then he saw the caravan in the distance. He knew that such caravans often bought slaves on their routes, and suddenly he realized what his brothers meant to do.

"Please don't," he begged them, but they were deaf to his pleas. They tied up his hands with the rope, and pulled him along to catch up to the caravan.

The leader of the caravan was a short, chubby man with a pointy black beard and fierce black eyes. He sized up Joseph very carefully. "What do you want for him?"

"He is strong and smart—he's worth thirty pieces of silver," said Simon. (Pieces of silver were the coins of the day—they looked liked silver dollars.)

"I'll give you ten," said the trader.

"Make it twenty and it's a sale," said Judah.

The trader nodded and paid up.

Gleefully, the brothers counted their coins, as poor Joseph was led off by the rope that tied his hands to a camel's saddle. Forlornly, he looked over his shoulder at his brothers. He couldn't believe what was happening to him. And then one of the slave traders yanked the rope and Joseph stumbled alongside the camel, which could move pretty fast on a flat surface.

After the caravan disappeared in the distance the brothers picked out a small goat from the flock and slashed its throat with a sharp knife. Blood gushed out. They took Joseph's coat and smeared it with the goat's blood.

Then they brought it to their father.

Jacob gasped, "Joseph's coat!"

Dan spoke up, pretending to be sad. "He must have been attacked by a wolf or a lion."

Jacob started to cry. His beloved son Joseph was dead—killed by a wild animal. For days he cried for his lost son, and even though the brothers started to feel bad, they never told him the truth.

Meanwhile, Joseph trudged along with the caravan in the direction of Egypt. Over and over again he asked, "Why? Why, God? Why?"

And then the answer came to him. He had been too

smug. He didn't consider his brothers' feelings as he pranced around in his fancy coat. He forgot to be grateful to God for the gifts he had received. He thought he was better than everybody else. He was insensitive. He exploited his father's admiration and love for him.

"Oh, God," he whispered. "Just give me a chance. I will change. I will make up for it. I promise."

And God heard his prayer.

After a long walk of many days, Joseph saw something strange in the distance—pointy objects that shone in the sunlight as if they were made of gold.

"What's that?" he asked one of the traders.

"Oh, those are pyramids," the trader said.

"What are pyramids?"

"Tombs for the dead rulers of Egypt. We are nearing the holy city of On, you know."

Joseph didn't know. This was all new to him. He asked many questions, which the trader seemed happy to answer. And so Joseph learned that unlike Hebron, where people were buried in caves, in Egypt the dead were dressed up in fancy outfits and put in houses built especially for them. These houses were called tombs, and the fanciest tombs were built for the dead pharaohs who were the kings of Egypt. The pyramids were huge—four hundred feet tall—and they were covered in shiny limestone plates, which made them glow in the sun as if they were made of gold. They looked magnificent. They are still standing today, and they still look magnificent, but all the limestone plates have been stolen long ago.

Joseph also learned that the holy city of On (the ruins of which still stand today, although its name has been changed to Heliopolis) was built at the very top of the Nile River that is known as the Nile delta.

"The holy city was built here because the Nile River is a god," said the trader.

"I don't get it," said Joseph, remembering everything he had learned from his father, Jacob, who learned it from his father, Isaac, who learned it from his father, Abraham. "How could a river be a god?"

The trader was surprised by the question. "It gives life to Egypt. Its water makes all the crops grow. Because of the Nile River, Egypt is a very rich country."

As the trader kept talking about the religious beliefs of Egypt, Joseph became more and more confused. How could the Egyptians believe that the Nile was a god? And that the sun was a god? And that bulls were gods? He didn't tell the trader that from his point of view none of this made any sense.

Soon, they could see the holy city of On up close.

Joseph gaped in wonder at the huge temples, which stood side by side, each dedicated to a different god. In front of each temple stood gigantic stone statues of people with animal heads—bulls, rams, crocodiles. They were supposed to be depictions of the gods. Joseph thought this was very weird.

All these temples needed lots of priests, the trader said. There were ten thousand priests who worked in On and many more slaves.

As the caravan wound through the streets, Joseph watched the goings-on. Men dressed in funny short skirts passed them by, some riding chariots drawn by horses, others walking along in leather boots that reached to their knees. It was hot in Egypt, and Joseph didn't understand why they wanted to wrap their legs with leather when you only needed to cover the bottoms of your feet to walk in comfort. But the trader explained, "Fine leather is expensive and high boots mean that the man is very wealthy."

"Oh," said Joseph, thinking that the Egyptians sure were strange.

The trader smiled at Joseph's bewildered expression. "I like you, kid," he said. "I think I will sell you to a very wealthy man. I want you to have a good life."

Joseph was very relieved to hear that. Ever since he

heard that many slaves worked in the temples, he was afraid he would be sold to a priest. And he knew that it would be an awful transgression against the one God to work around idols. Didn't his great-grandfather Abraham destroy all the idols in the idol shop when he was a boy? He said a silent prayer to God for sparing him such a fate.

The kind trader sold Joseph to a man named Potiphar. Mr. Potiphar was a very rich man, and he had a beautiful house of many rooms decorated with tile pictures, called mosaics. His house was surrounded with gardens full of flowers, and beyond them were vineyards overflowing with grapes to be made into wine, and orchards full of oranges, peaches, olives, and pomegranates. It was a huge place and Joseph could see that many slaves were needed to keep it running.

Joseph was assigned to work in the orchard watering

the trees. He and other slaves carried big jugs of water all day long and emptied them under the trees. It was very hard work, and at first Joseph hurt all over. He didn't know which hurt worse—his sore muscles or his broken heart. He missed his father and he was very, very sad each time he remembered what his brothers did to him.

One day, as he was carrying his hundredth jug of water, he decided to say something to the foreman who told the slaves what to do and who carried a whip to hit any slave that might try slowing down on the job.

"Sir," he said very politely. "Why don't we just dig long ditches from the well to the trees and fill them with water? That way the water can run down all by itself, and we won't have to work so hard all day long."

The foreman immediately grew angry at the suggestion. "You lazy slave! I'll give you five lashes for trying to get out of work."

"No, no, please don't. I was just—"

But the foreman didn't want to hear what Joseph had to say, and he raised his whip.

But just then a loud voice shouted, "STOP!" It was Mr. Potiphar. He had overheard Joseph.

"Young man," said Mr. Potiphar. "I like that idea. You are very smart. Do you have any other ideas that would make my house run more efficiently?"

Joseph did. Mr. Potiphar was very interested and pretty soon Joseph was trying out all sorts of experiments in the vineyards and orchards.

Of course, Joseph *was* very smart and—let's not forget—he had a special gift to be the best at everything he tried. Very soon, Mr. Potiphar made him foreman.

Years passed. Joseph grew up. He had learned a lot by his experiences and now he was humble. He never told any of the slaves that he was better than they were. He showed them respect at all times. As a result, they showed him respect in return, and the Potiphar household was a happy place.

All this did not escape Mr. Potiphar. Eventually, Joseph was given the responsibility for the whole household, and with it was given a very special mark of distinction. Even though Joseph was still a slave, he didn't have to wear the brown slave's tunic anymore. Instead, he got a special red coat that symbolized that he was in charge. It was not as beautiful as the coat of many colors his father gave him, but it was nice. When Joseph looked at it, he felt proud and sad at the same time. Proud that his master trusted and appreciated him, and sad because he remembered how much his father had loved him and the beautiful coat that would never be his again.

God had given Joseph many gifts, among them was good looks. If Joseph were alive today he could be a model or a movie star. Now, in his red robe, he looked especially handsome.

Mrs. Potiphar became aware of this attractive member of her household when, one day, he reported to her on a matter of flowers from the garden. From then on, she would send for him just because she liked him. Often, she would say, "Why don't you rest and have a cup of tea with me."

Joseph felt guilty about sitting drinking tea while the other slaves were working so hard, and he also thought that maybe Mr. Potiphar wouldn't like it. So he thanked Mrs. Potiphar for being so nice and went back to his work.

The more Joseph declined Mrs. Potiphar's invitations, the more determined she became to have him like her. "You're such a good-looking man," she told him, and Joseph became very embarrassed. She was a married woman! She was his master's wife!

By now, Mrs. Potiphar was becoming desperate. She had to catch Joseph's attention one way or the other.

And then she saw her chance. A special holiday was coming up honoring the god of the Nile River, and Mr. Potiphar and the entire household would be there to participate in the celebration. Of course, Joseph wouldn't go, because he believed in the one God and he knew that it was wrong to worship idols.

Mrs. Potiphar decided to stay home too. She told her husband she had a headache and couldn't go out. She would be alone with Joseph at last.

Everyone left and now the house was empty. She summoned Joseph to her bedroom. "Oh, I feel so bad, my head hurts so much," she moaned, lying in bed.

"I'm sorry, Mrs. Potiphar. Is there anything I can do?"

"Yes, feel my forehead. . . . Do I have a fever?"

Joseph did as he was told. And when he bent over, she threw her arms around his neck and kissed him.

Startled, Joseph jumped back, but she held onto his coat.

"Don't be afraid," she purred. "Everyone is gone."

"No, no . . . this is wrong. I cannot betray my master," Joseph said. And he rushed out of the room, leaving her holding his red coat.

Mrs. Potiphar was very angry. No slave was going to reject her! He had to be punished for this.

When her husband returned from the celebration, he found her lying in bed, crying her eyes out and holding Joseph's coat.

"What happened?" Mr. Potiphar asked.

"How could you do this to me?" she sobbed.

"What are you talking about?"

"That terrible Joseph, whom you put in charge, thinks now everything belongs to him, including his master's wife!"

"What?"

"Yes, he came to my room and tried to kiss me. When he heard you coming, he ran away so fast, he left his coat. See, I have it right here."

Mr. Potiphar said nothing but looked at his wife with piercing eyes. He knew her well. He knew her tears were false.

"Are you sure this is how it happened?" he asked.

"Are you calling me a liar?" Mrs. Potiphar shrieked. "Are you defending a slave?"

Mr. Potiphar knew that Joseph could never be guilty of this crime. But he also knew that in Egypt it was law that a slave's word could never be taken over that of an Egyptian citizen. So he was stuck. Softly, he said, "I'll deal with him."

A crime such as Mrs. Potiphar described was punishable by death. But Mr. Potiphar felt that this would be too unjust. Therefore, he commanded that Joseph be thrown in prison—at least his life would be spared.

He was very sorry to lose the best worker he ever had, but this was the only thing he could do under the circumstances.

For the second time in his life, Joseph was bewildered. Again, he asked, "Why? Why, God? Why?" And the answer that came to him was that he had to know what it feels like to be wrongly accused. He had wrongly accused his brothers of not watching the sheep and of saying mean things, when they weren't guilty.

He was very sorry for the things he had said. And while he was in prison he thought about all the things he had done wrong. He prayed to God, promising he would be a better person.

This is why Joseph is a hero. He had done things wrong, but when bad things happened to him, he didn't just moan and groan. He asked himself why he was being punished. And he saw how he had contributed to his own misfortune. Then he was sorry and he resolved to be better. Only a hero tries to be good even when bad things are happening to him.

There is a very interesting end to Joseph's story.

While he was in prison, he became famous for interpreting the dreams of other prisoners. This reputation reached the ears of the pharaoh of Egypt, who had just had a troubling dream. Joseph interpreted the dream as a warning that a famine was coming. A famine is when there is no food, and it happens when there is no rain for a long time and things can't grow.

The pharaoh was upset at the news. "A famine? That can't happen to Egypt! What can I do to prevent it?"

Joseph explained—because he was very smart, smarter even than the pharaoh—that they should immediately start stocking up a lot of food, so that when the famine came, they would have things to eat. The pharaoh was very impressed. He said, "You have saved Egypt. I will make you my chief advisor."

Joseph was appointed a grand vizier—that is what advisors to the pharaoh were called—and was given a beautiful colorful coat embroidered with gold thread that marked his new rank.

Coats always seemed to play an important part in the life of Joseph. This one was even more beautiful than the coat his father gave him long ago, but when he put it on he felt sad. He wished he was back home with his father and his brothers. He missed them all.

And then a fantastic thing happened. When the famine hit, his brothers came to Egypt to buy food. Because Joseph was dressed in his Egyptian costume, they didn't recognize him when they bowed to the grand vizier of Egypt (just like his dreams of long ago predicted they would). But Joseph recognized them.

He decided to see if they had changed any and, perhaps, like him, had been sorry for what they did and become better people. So he put them through a test, and he saw that they all had changed. As a matter of fact, Judah, the brother who was the nastiest, was the best. He was willing to be put in prison rather than hurt any of his brothers or father.

So then, Joseph told them who he was. Boy, were they surprised! He hugged them and everybody cried with happiness.

Then Joseph invited them all to live with him in Egypt where there was plenty of food. They went back and got their father, who cried when he learned that his favorite son was still alive. (There was a lot of crying and hugging going on, I can tell you that.)

And that's how the whole family settled in Egypt.

But living in Egypt turned out to be not so good. To find out why, you have to read the next story.

CHAPTER 4

SISTER, SISTER

*The Story of Miriam and How She Risked
Her Life for Her Baby Brother*

THE FAMILY OF Joseph came to live with him in
Egypt. It was a large group. There was Joseph's
father, Jacob, whose name God had changed to
Israel—God often changed the names of special people
in the Bible. There were all of Israel's sons, who were,
of course, Joseph's brothers. There were all their
wives and sons and daughters, who, by now, were
married and had sons and daughters of their own.
Seventy people in all. Because they were descendants
of Israel, they became known in Egypt as the
Israelites.

Joseph was very happy to help his family. He made
sure they had plenty to eat during the famine and a
nice place to live. He settled them at the top of the
Nile River (not too far from Heliopolis) in an area
called Goshen. Joseph had traveled through there
when he first arrived in Egypt as a slave on a spice
caravan; he remembered those beautiful fertile fields and

fruitful orchards and fragrant gardens.

Why was it so special? Because of the Nile River.

The Nile spills over its banks once a year. If that happened in America, it would be called a flood and the place declared a disaster area. But the Egyptians were delighted, because when the Nile spilled over its bank, it deposited a rich mud that was very good for growing things. Joseph made sure that his people, the Israelites, lived in the muddiest place of all. (When I was a kid, I loved playing in the mud, so I would have liked living there.)

Because of the mud, their fields yielded large crops. And soon they all became very wealthy. They had nice houses, made of mud bricks, and they were very happy. They felt they were blessed by God. Not only did they have large crops, but their sheep and goats and camels munched the rich grass and had many offspring, so their flocks grew. And best of all, their families also grew. All the Israelite families had many children.

Everything was great. One hundred years passed. Then two hundred. Now, there were millions of Israelites living in Egypt.

And then things started to go wrong. The Egyptians began to feel that there were too many of them.

The Israelites stuck out among the Egyptians because they were so different. They still dressed in robes, the way their grandfathers had dressed; they never picked up the Egyptian fashion of wearing short skirts and leather boots. They still spoke Hebrew—the language of Abraham, Isaac, and Jacob. And they still called themselves by their Hebrew names, which sounded very strange to the Egyptians.

When the Israelites noticed that they were being eyed with suspicion, they got worried. "Let's show our loyalty to Egypt," they told each other. "Let's prove to the Egyptians that we are good citizens." They started to worship the Egyptian gods—like the bull god, Baal, or the sheep god, Amon, or the lion goddess, Sekmet.

At first, it was just for show. They didn't really mean it; they still believed in the one God. But, after they had worshiped these idols for a while, the Israelites began to forget about the one God Abraham had discovered long ago.

When the Israelites forgot about God and all the great things He had done for them, the Egyptians forgot about Joseph and all the great things he had done for them too.

Reading about this in Sunday school, I knew the Israelites had it coming. I noticed that things go bad in the Bible when people forget about God. That's just how it is!

And sure enough, a new pharaoh came to the throne and he started asking: "Who are these strange people?

What are they doing in my country?"

Everyone, it seems, had forgotten about the famine and how Joseph had saved Egypt from starvation and been named grand vizier, and how he had brought his family over there.

The pharaoh began to distrust the Israelites. Suppose there was a war with another big empire—the Assyrians or the Hittites, who were making noises in the north— would these strange people side with Egypt or join the enemy? He considered throwing the Israelites out of the country, but there were so many of them and they were all very rich. He didn't want this large group of hard workers to leave and take their riches with them. So he devised a secret plan to make sure that the Israelites would never pose a threat.

He announced a huge building project right at the top of the Nile. Two new cities were to be built with many temples and tombs. All citizens of the area were called upon to volunteer in the construction. Naturally, the Israelites rushed right over to show their loyalty. And when they did, they found soldiers with whips and chains waiting for them.

Oh yes, they would build the new cities for the pharaoh—the magnificent cities of Pithom and Raamses. But they would build them as slaves. They cried and begged for mercy, but the Egyptian taskmasters just beat them with whips. It was terrible.

They were forced to scoop up mud to make bricks for building the huge monuments. They had to haul heavy rocks. They had to work in the dirt all day long.

The pharaoh was pleased with himself. The Israelites would be no threat if they were oppressed. But it still worried him that they were having a lot of children. *Little boys can grow up to be soldiers,* he thought. (They didn't have female soldiers back then like we have today.) So he ordered all newborn Israelite boys killed.

When the edict went out, the Israelite mothers sobbed all night long. How horrible to give birth to a new baby—an occasion for much happiness—only to have that helpless little thing murdered.

I remember when my youngest sister, Ruth, was born; she was so tiny and red and helpless. Even though I really wanted a baby brother, I couldn't help but like her anyway. I just wanted to cuddle her and wrap her in a warm blanket. Can you imagine anyone wanting to hurt a tiny baby like that?

But the Egyptians were very cruel. They didn't care about the Israelite babies. They didn't care about the pain and sadness of the parents who lost their children in this horrible way. They couldn't care less.

One Israelite mother and father, who already had a three-year-old son named Aaron and a five-year-old daughter named Miriam, sat down to talk about what they should do.

"There is only one thing we can do," said the father. "We must get a divorce."

"A divorce?" asked little Miriam, who was always listening to everything.

"Yes," said her mother. "Your father is right. We have to get a divorce. If we stay married, we might have another baby—and if it's a boy, he will be murdered." And she began to sob.

But little Miriam didn't cry. She thought about it for a while and then she said, "I'm sorry Mom and Dad, but I think you are doing a very bad thing."

"No, sweetheart," said her father patiently. "The Egyptians are doing a bad thing."

"But, Dad, what you are doing is worse."

"Worse?" Her mother was so shocked by little Miriam's words that she stopped crying. "How can you say such a thing?"

"Yes, it's worse. The Egyptians don't have anything against baby girls. But if you get a divorce, there will be no hope for baby boys *or* baby girls to be born."

Miriam was right! There wouldn't be any baby boys or girls. When I read that in Sunday school, I couldn't wait to run home and tell my six sisters that if they were living at that time, they wouldn't have been born. They didn't like hearing it at all. My sister Betty stuck her tongue out at me and said, "You wouldn't have been born either, stupid." And my big sister Miriam—yes, I had a sister named Miriam too— tattled to my mother that I was saying mean things.

Miriam's parents (I mean those in the Bible, not my parents) thought about what their little daughter had said. They realized she was very wise even though she was so young. They decided not to get a divorce.

Pretty soon, the Egyptians got tired of killing the babies and things went back to normal. That is, the Israelites were still slaves, and they still had to work very hard. But at least, there wasn't the daily crying of mothers whose babies had been murdered.

Then Miriam's mother got pregnant. And, for a tiny moment she was very happy. But then more terrible news hit.

It began when the pharaoh had a dream. (And, as we know from the story of Joseph, the pharaohs considered their dreams to be very important.) This dream was more like a nightmare, and it scared the pharaoh very much. The dream seemed to be suggesting that all of Egypt would be destroyed by one man. He immediately sent for his advisors. "Explain it to me right now—what does this dream mean?" he demanded.

The advisors called in astrologers—the people who look at the stars and make predictions from their movements and patterns. They deliberated in hushed tones for days—everyone was afraid of making a mistake and giving the pharaoh wrong advice.

Finally, the pharaoh lost his temper. "Stop whispering and tell me what this is all about!" he shouted.

The astrologers didn't know for sure what the pharaoh's dream meant, but they had a good idea. And here is what they said: "Your most high majesty . . . the stars tell us that very soon an Israelite baby boy will be born. He will have the power to destroy Egypt."

"Impossible!" yelled the pharaoh. "We are the mightiest empire on earth! The Israelites are our slaves! They are nothing! They can't destroy Egypt!"

The astrologers started to scurry away, afraid that the pharaoh's fury would soon be unleashed and he might order them killed. But one of the astrologers, a nasty, evil man named Bilam, spoke right up to the pharaoh. "Your most high majesty, the stars not only tell us what the problem is, but how to fix it."

The pharaoh calmed down a little. "Well, why didn't you tell me that in the first place," he huffed.

"Allow me to explain it now."

"Speak!" the pharaoh ordered.

"The stars tell us that this Israelite baby boy, who will have the power to destroy Egypt, has one weakness."

"What is it? I want to know right now! What is his weakness?" shouted the pharaoh.

When I read this in Sunday school, I could see the guy was losing it. Some pharaoh. Kings and presidents are supposed to behave with dignity. But then what could you expect from a guy who enslaved an entire nation of people and ordered their tiny helpless babies murdered? I couldn't wait to get through the story to find out how God got even with him!

Bilam was very crafty. The stars did indeed show

something about a weakness, but it wasn't clear. So Bilam decided to make up something that would satisfy the pharaoh. Bilam was greedy. He was already counting in his head the great honors he would receive for his advice. After all, when Joseph interpreted the pharaoh's dream long ago, he was named grand vizier.

"Speak up!" the pharaoh was yelling. "Tell me the secret of his weakness!"

"Water."

"Water?"

"Yes, your majesty. His weakness is water."

"What does that mean?"

"Your majesty, you can destroy this baby boy with water."

"How do I do that?"

Bilam smiled. *How smart I am,* he thought. And he presented his evil plan. "Your majesty, the most powerful god of Egypt is the Nile River. Let the water of the Nile consume the destroyer of Egypt. Throw all newborn Israelite boy babies in the river and you will be rid of the problem."

"It shall be done!" declared the pharaoh, happy at last that he had an answer to his nightmare.

When the decree was announced among the Israelites, there was heartbreak and sobbing all over again. The one who cried the hardest was Miriam's mother, because she had just given birth to a beautiful baby boy. She named the tiny boy Yekusiel, which means "hope in God," because she hoped that God would save him somehow.

At any moment the Egyptians could find out about the baby and a death squad would come and take him away to be thrown into the Nile.

It was going to take a miracle to save him. And a miracle came— in the form of an idea. Miriam's idea.

"Mom," she said, "I know a place, a little cave near the river, where we can hide him."

Her mother was willing to try anything. In the dark of night, they took the tiny baby to the cave and fixed it up like a little nursery with colorful blankets and a small basket that would be little Yekusiel's crib. At

night his mother would sleep with him. During the day, Miriam would stay in the cave playing with her baby brother and rocking him gently. (My sister Miriam would never have done that for me.)

Yekusiel was a wonderful baby, alert and happy, smiling sweetly at his sister. He hardly ever cried, though sometimes Miriam would have to put her hand over his little mouth to stop his gurgling when she thought she heard someone coming.

All the while, the killing of the infants continued. The Egyptian soldiers would come to an Israelite house, kick in the door, and grab the babies right from their mothers' arms. If the baby was a girl, they'd give it back to the mother and walk out, and not even say, "Sorry to disturb you." But if it was a boy, they'd take that little baby and leave, while the mother screamed, "Please don't do this! Please don't kill my baby!" They would take that helpless little thing to the river, throw it in, and laugh.

While this was going on, for three months Miriam and her mother kept little Yekusiel in the cave. But they could not hide him there much longer. For one thing, it was not good for him to be in the dark all the time—his mother worried that he might go blind. He was already very pale from not getting any sun. But also, as he was growing, he was beginning to laugh out loud and squeal with delight—particularly when little Miriam brought some shiny stones for him to play with. And he was beginning to vocalize sounds like "Mi Mi" when he saw Miriam and "Ma Ma" when he saw his mother. Soon, someone would hear him and that would be the end.

Miriam thought and thought. What could she do to help her baby brother? One day, while sitting at the opening of the cave and watching the river flowing down below, she started to pray to God.

"Dear God, I know in my heart this baby is special. When he grows up, he will do great things. But not if he dies. Help us, please. Save my little baby brother. I trust in you and hope with every ounce of my strength that you will. Thank you God."

God heard her and answered her prayers.

My Sunday-school teacher told us that God hears everybody's prayers and that He answers them all. But a lot of the times, the answer is no. Well, Miriam got a yes.

As Miriam was praying, she saw a piece of drift-wood floating on the river. The wood did not sink. *Of course!* thought Miriam. You guessed it—Miriam got another great idea. That Miriam was one smart cookie! But she did have the help of God.

When her mother came to the cave that night, Miriam presented her plan. Her mother was not as thrilled about it as Miriam, but when Miriam told her that she came up with it while praying, her mother decided to take it seriously. Maybe it was a special sign from God that Miriam's idea would work. The next day she put Miriam's plan into action. And this is what she did.

She took the little basket that was Yekusiel's crib and plugged up all the holes with clay. To make doubly sure that no water could get in, she painted the outside with tar, the thick black oily stuff we cover our roads with. Now, she was sure that the basket would float on the river. With tears in her eyes, she put the gurgling baby inside.

"Don't worry, Mom," said Miriam. "It will work. He will float right out of Egypt, where some nice fisherman who never heard of the pharaoh's decree will take him home. Just have hope in God."

Her mother nodded. Hadn't she named her baby "hope in God"? Well, now was the time to have that hope.

She kissed Yekusiel and gently covered him with a thin linen cloth so his pale skin wouldn't get burned in the hot sun. Then with a deep ache in her heart, she placed the basket with the baby in the Nile River. She watched the current swirl around it and carry it away. Then she broke down sobbing.

But, as usual, Miriam did not cry. Miriam was watching the basket on the water, and when she saw it moving farther away, she decided to follow it.

"No, don't go," said her mother. "You might walk onto Egyptian property and get in trouble. I don't want to lose two of my children in one day."

"I'll only go a little way," said Miriam firmly. "Have hope, Mom."

Her mother didn't stop her anymore and Miriam walked along the river, keeping her eyes on the basket.

In the beginning it moved rapidly with the current, but then it came to a place where the Nile widened and the shallow parts of the river near the banks were overgrown with reeds with brown fuzzy tops (which today we call cattails). The basket floated among the reeds, bouncing off their thick stalks. Momentarily, Miriam felt relieved. She had been afraid she couldn't keep up with the fast-moving water, and she was glad the progress of the basket had slowed down. But then she realized where she was, and she got scared again.

The basket had wandered into a part of the Nile River that was especially holy to the Egyptians. Here, the sacred ceremonies were carried out at flood time by the Egyptian priests. This was where the pharaoh and his court came to bathe, a place that was totally off-limits to everyone else. The tall reeds obscured her view, but she knew that there were royal guards posted in this area and soon they might spot her. She looked down at the basket. It was floating ever so slowly now. She had a little time to think, pray, and figure out what to do.

But before she had a chance to come up with a plan, she heard voices. They were coming toward her!

Quickly, she stepped into the river. She waded among the reeds. She would hide there until the voices passed.

The voices grew louder, and now, an incredible

procession appeared in view. Wow, Miriam had never seen anything like it. Her eyes opened wide.

First came the royal guards in their leather helmets with feathers on top, and dressed in leather skirts and leather boots. They all carried spears. Then came the palace servants in very pretty blue robes, waving palm branches to keep the air cool. Then came the hand-maidens in vividly colored dresses and wearing many bracelets and necklaces of shiny beads. And in the middle of the handmaidens walked a young woman who was dressed all in gold. She had a gold circle on her head with a gold snake protruding from it. That was the crown of the royal family of Egypt. This was the princess! The daughter of the pharaoh! She had come to bathe in the river.

Miriam kept one eye on the basket, which had gotten stuck between densely growing reeds, and another on the princess. She was afraid that little Yekusiel might start to cry and be discovered. But she was also fascinated by what she was seeing.

The guards erected a tent for the princess and moved off into the distance to give her privacy. Miriam was greatly relieved; if the guards had found the baby in the basket, they would have drowned it for sure.

The princess was taking off her crown and her many gold bracelets and necklaces. She was just about ready to take off her dress, when she lifted her head and listened. Baby Yekusiel had whimpered in his basket; the noise of the voices must have awakened him. "Oh no," Miriam gasped. Silently she prayed, "Dear God, please keep him quiet." And God answered her prayers, but this time He said no.

The baby whimpered again and everybody heard it.

"That sounds like a little baby," the princess said.

"Your majesty, what would a baby be doing here?" one of the handmaidens asked. "That could be a crocodile snorkeling in the water."

Oh, good, thought Miriam, *maybe they'll get scared and leave.*

But the princess said, "Nonsense, the crocodiles live downriver." She peered through the reeds and saw the basket. "What's that?"

"Oh, that's just an old basket," the handmaiden replied.

"Go, bring it," the princess commanded. "I want to see what's inside."

Miriam clasped her hand over her mouth and prayed as hard as she knew how. The baby would be discovered any second now by the daughter of the same pharaoh who ordered all Israelite boys be drowned. Oh, dear God!

The handmaiden assigned to the task was clearly not happy about wading in the water to get some stupid old basket. She couldn't understand why the princess wanted it at all. So she took her time tying up her dress so it wouldn't get wet, hoping the princess's attention would be diverted by something else. But the princess just waited patiently. So, having no other choice, the handmaiden waded in. Holding onto the reeds, she made her way toward the basket. The water was deeper there and her dress got wet after all.

"Yuk," she said, "it's covered with icky black stuff."

Miriam had another small wave of hope that none of them would want to touch the tar and give up. But then she heard the princess say sweetly, "Never mind your complaining. Just bring it to me."

The princess really did sound like a nice person, not like the pharaoh's daughter at all. I mean, if you were royalty and you issued a command, you might get very mad that somebody was taking such a long time to obey you.

Meanwhile, the handmaiden made her way back, still trying to hold up her soaked dress with one hand, while pushing the basket along the water with the other.

Now she really had no choice—she had to pick up the black sticky thing, but she set the basket down on the ground in front of the princess as fast as she could.

With a look of great anticipation, the princess lifted the linen cover from the basket and gasped in delight. "Oh, what a beautiful little baby boy."

Yekusiel was crying softly, his tears running down his pale little cheeks.

The handmaidens all crowded around the basket and Miriam couldn't see a thing.

"It's an Israelite baby, your majesty!" one of the handmaidens exclaimed. "He is supposed to be drowned!"

"Oh, he is the sweetest baby I ever saw," the princess was saying. She really did sound like a very good woman.

But the handmaiden had evil in her heart. "Your majesty, you can't feel sorry for him," she insisted. "Your father issued the death decree on all the Israelite baby boys. We have to call the guards and have him drowned. We can't disobey the pharaoh!"

Miriam's heart was beating so loud, she could hardly hear what the princess said in reply. She had to do something drastic. She stepped out of her reed hiding place. "Your majesty!" she called out.

They all turned around in surprise. What was this slave girl doing here?

"I know what happened with this baby," Miriam announced, her knees trembling under her slave robe, which was all wet anyway.

The baby quieted down, reassured by his sister's voice.

"You do?" The princess smiled at her. She had a very kind face, and she looked much less threatening without the snake crown on her head. "Please tell me."

"I was watching what happened. The guards threw this baby into the river to drown him," Miriam lied, beads of sweat standing out on her forehead. "But the god of the Nile picked him up and let him float on top of the holy water. The god of the Nile didn't want to consume this baby because he is special." Of course, Miriam didn't believe that there was such a thing as the god of the Nile, she was just making up a story that she hoped would save her brother.

The princess clapped her hands together, very happy to hear Miriam's story. "Yes, you are so right. If the god of the Nile wanted to consume him, this child would have drowned. But he is alive." She turned to the handmaidens. "You see, the god of the Nile sent this baby to me as a present. I have no children, and the god of the Nile has answered my prayers for a little baby boy all of my own!"

"But, your majesty, what about your father?" The nasty handmaiden wasn't giving up.

The princess scowled for the first time. She stamped her foot. "Don't you know that the pharaoh is a god himself. He speaks to the other gods all the time. I am sure he knows all about it."

Of course, the pharaoh wasn't a god any more than the river was a god, but he just told people that to make them afraid of him. Would he admit that the god of the Nile didn't tell him about the baby? For sure not.

The princess smiled and again turned to Miriam. "What's your name, little girl?"

"Miriam."

"Pleased to meet you, Miriam. My name is Batya."

Batya? Miriam was very surprised to hear it. *Batya meant "daughter of God." Maybe she was really an angel,* Miriam thought, *sent from heaven to rescue Yekusiel.*

(I guess Miriam was never told angels are invisible.)

"And speaking of names," the princess said, "we have to name this tiny one." She patted his little head. "I think I will call you Moses."

"Moses? But his—" Miriam blurted out.

"What did you say?" The princess turned to her.

"Oh, I never heard that name before," Miriam corrected herself. She couldn't tell the princess this was her baby brother and he already had a name.

"Moses means 'from the water,'" the princess explained. "I will call him my 'water baby.'" She laughed in delight and picked up the baby from the basket. Immediately he started to cry.

"Oh, dear, dear." The princess was concerned.

Miriam wanted to say, "Here, give him to me," but she didn't want to press her luck any further. Yekusiel—now Moses—was such a good, quiet baby, he wouldn't cry long.

"But, your majesty," another handmaiden spoke

up. "None of us here knows how to take care of a baby, how to change diapers or feed him."

"We must find a nanny," the princess declared.

Miriam took a deep breath. "Your majesty, I know where there is a nanny."

"You do, Miriam?"

"Yes, your majesty."

"Well, suppose you go get her."

Miriam turned around and ran as fast as her feet could carry her. She was completely breathless when she finally got home. "Mom . . . mom," she could barely get the words out. "Guess what happened?"

Her mother could hardly believe the story. But she followed Miriam as they ran back to the princess, who was still trying to soothe the crying baby.

"Your majesty, . . ." Miriam was panting. "I found you a nanny."

The princess Batya smiled her kindly smile. "Can you take care of a tiny baby like this?" she asked.

"Yes." Miriam's mother was very relieved by the princess's kindness. "May I show you how?" She reached for her son and, of course, when he felt the comforting arms of his mother, Moses stopped crying immediately.

"You seem to be an excellent nanny," said the

princess. "I want you to take care of my baby."

"Your baby?"

The words just slipped out. But the mother recovered quickly. "Oh, your majesty, I will take care of him as if he were my own."

Miriam was a little sad as she watched the procession depart for the palace, her mother clutching little Moses. But she knew she had saved her baby brother.

Yes, Miriam was a real hero. When everyone despaired, even her parents, she thought clearly. She never forgot that at the worst of times, when all seems lost, it is very important to have hope in God, because God takes care of all the people that trust in him.

Still, it was not easy to risk her life and step out of her hiding place in the reeds to speak to the princess. For all she knew, the princess—who was, after all, the daughter of the cruel pharaoh—would order her killed. But Miriam was brave. She put her love for her baby brother ahead of any fear of punishment, even death.

They don't make heroes any better than that.

Even though Miriam knew her baby brother was living the life of a prince in the palace, she felt sad because she missed him so much. She wondered if she would ever see him again. She'd try to catch glimpses of him whenever the pharaoh and his family went on parade. She wondered if they would ever play together.

But Miriam was also patient. And she prayed and waited, hoping that that special moment would come someday.

Miriam grew up and so did Moses. And then Moses left the palace and saw how horribly the Israelite slaves were treated. In his heart, he knew that they were his people.

So Moses rebelled against the pharaoh, and with the help of God, he freed all the slaves. God sent plagues that nearly destroyed Egypt, and that helped a lot. The plagues were really awful—first the Nile River turned to blood, then the whole place was over-run by frogs, then by bugs called locusts. But pharaoh continued to be stubborn. And finally all the first-born Egyptian boys died. That's when the pharaoh realized that he couldn't fight God any longer, and he let the Israelites leave.

So, Moses led all the Israelites out of Egypt. Of course, Miriam was right there, looking after him and cheering him on.

Moses was a superhero, and Miriam was so proud of him. Her little baby brother became one of the most famous men in the history of civilization.

The astrologers were right—he was that special baby with the God-given power to intimidate the mightiest empire on earth.

After the Israelites escaped from Egypt, they came to a mountain called Mount Sinai, and Moses went to the top and got the Ten Commandments, straight from God.

Wow!

But waiting for him down below, the impatient Israelites fell back on their old habits. They built an Egyptian-style idol to worship—a golden calf—which for sure little Abram would have destroyed if it was in his father's shop.

Now, I will let you in on a secret. It was only the adults who built this idol. The kids weren't involved. They knew the adults were just playing with a big toy—and that toy couldn't be God.

When Moses came down from the mountain, he went ballistic. Even Miriam couldn't calm him down. What happened next is a long story, but in the end everybody apologized to God and started walking through the desert, making their way back to their home in Canaan.

They got lost a lot, and it took them forty years to get there. But finally, they were home, in Canaan, now

Israel, which was promised by God to their great-great-grandfathers Abraham, Isaac, and Jacob; that's why they also called it the Promised Land.

You'd think that would be the end of their problems. Oh no, another empire—the Philistine—was just itching to conquer the Israelites and make them slaves again.

What happened?

It's in the next story.

CHAPTER 5

THE TRUE ORIGINS OF RUBBER BANDS AND SPITBALLS

*The Story of David
and His Bag of Pebbles*

WHEN I WAS A KID, I had a slingshot. If you never had one, let me tell you what it looks like. It's a twig in the shape of the letter Y. I had to look real hard to find the right kind of twig—it had to be about the size of my hand, and strong. (I broke it off from a neighbor's apple tree, but my sister Betty saw me and tattled to my mother and I got in trouble. So I don't recommend getting yours that way.)

Once I found the right twig, I tied a rubber band to the two tall parts of the Y. When I pulled back on the rubber band, it had a good snap. Then I made a spitball from a piece of paper I chewed on and spit out. I put the spitball into the rubber band and let 'er fly. I meant to hit my friend Pete, who was sitting across from me in Sunday school, but I hit the teacher instead, and boy did I ever get in trouble! They took my slingshot away from me, and I had to stay after school. (My sister Betty said, "I told you so," which I hated most of all.)

The only good part was that my teacher decided to use that opportunity to tell us about the famous boy hero of the Bible who had a slingshot. Well, he didn't really have a slingshot; he had a sling, which doesn't use a rubber band, but it kind of works the same. This story became the most favorite of my favorite stories. Let me tell it to you now.

The Israelites finally got back home to the Promised Land, which they called Israel. But, it wasn't empty; it was full of people who didn't want them back. The worst were a nasty, mean people called the Philistines, who lived along the coast of the Mediterranean Sea— in the cities of Gaza, Ashdod, and Ashkelon, which are still there today.

When the Philistines saw the Israelites moving into the neighborhood, they wanted to kill them.

The Philistines were very strong—they had the secret of melting iron and making iron tools. They thought they were the strongest people on earth, even stronger than God.

Well, when I read that in Sunday school, I knew what was coming next. God was going to teach them a lesson. Because nobody is stronger than God.

Meanwhile, the Israelites weren't doing too well in the God department themselves. They knew God's commandments—they got them at Mount Sinai—but they had trouble keeping them. Their victories and defeats depended on how well they were doing keeping God's commandments. If they were good, God helped them, and they always won. If they were bad, God wouldn't help them, and sometimes they were lucky and won, but most of the time they lost miserably.

The Israelites had a king named Saul. He had a hard time fighting the nations that attacked the Israelites like the Amalekites and the Philistines.

During this time, in the town of Bethlehem (which means "house of bread"), there lived a man named Jesse.

When I read that, I guessed right away that they called the town the house of bread, because it had a lot of bakeries in it. My teacher said I was right. But I wondered if they also had cheese and milk there, or did you have to go to other places called the "house of cheese" and the "house of milk" to get them? (If that's how it worked, I would have lived in the "house of chocolate.") I asked my teacher, but she said no. Only the places most famous for their products were named like that, and they didn't have any chocolate back then in Israel. (Chocolate comes from cacao, which grows in South America, and America hadn't been discovered yet.)

Jesse was from the tribe of Judah—Judah, you remember, was a brother of Joseph and one of the twelve sons of Jacob. (All the descendants of Judah were called Jews.) Jesse had eight sons. The eighth, the youngest and the smallest, was David.

His older brothers were all drafted into the king's army, so David—too young to be a soldier—had to go tend his father's flock of sheep. Of course, David wanted to go with his brothers and fight the Philistines too, but his father said, "You're too small, David; I need you to stay and watch the sheep in the field." So David had to obey his father.

David was a gentle boy, not at all like his warrior brothers. In fact, his father hoped that the war would be over soon, because he didn't want David to be drafted too. He thought that such a boy didn't stand a chance in the army. They'd probably make him the cook or messenger or something very unheroic.

Besides being the smallest, David stood out in other ways. The Bible tells us he was handsome, with beautiful eyes and red hair. When his brothers wanted to tease him they called him "carrottop." But he was very good-natured and he didn't mind. He just laughed.

When his brothers went to war, David took the sheep up into the mountains, high above Bethlehem, where the grass was green and tender. During the day, he watched over his sheep to make sure none of them got lost, and in the evening, when the sheep were fed and going to sleep, he would look at the sky scattered with a million twinkling stars and think about who put them up there. He knew it was God.

Another young boy might be scared being alone all night, but not David. That was because David felt that God was always close by. He just knew that God was with him, and since God was more powerful than anything on earth, that meant that nothing could harm him.

Whenever David felt the slightest bit afraid in the dark, he would think about God, and he'd feel much better right away. During these moments, he would often be filled with an overwhelming feeling of gratitude and love toward God. Then he would pull out a small harp that his father had given him. It had eight strings stretched tight on a wooden bow, and when you strummed the strings with your fingers, it made a beautiful sound. He would play the harp and sing a song that he made up on the spot.

David's best songs have been collected in the Bible. They are called Psalms. The one everyone knows goes like this:

> *The Lord is my shepherd;*
> *I shall not want.*
> *He makes me lie down in green pastures;*
> *He leads me beside quiet waters;*
> *He renews my life;*
> *He guides me to the right paths*
> *   for His name's sake.*
> *Even though I walk through the valley of*
> *   deepest darkness, I fear no harm,*
> *Because You are with me . . .*

When he sang these songs nobody heard him, except his flocks and the wild animals in the forest and, of course, God.

The mountains, where David was pasturing his sheep, were in the real wilderness. There were many hungry lions and bears lurking about, all thinking that it might be nice to have lamb chops for dinner.

David had to be alert at all times, or one of his sheep might fall into the claws of a dangerous predator. For this reason, he carried a sling.

As I said, the sling was a little different from a slingshot. In those days rubber bands hadn't been invented yet. (No chocolate and no rubber bands—life sure was tough back then.) Without a rubber band you had to get the snap a different way.

Here's how it worked: There was a shallow leather bowl, where you put a pebble, or a rock (if you really intended to do some damage). The bowl had two long leather straps attached to it. One strap you tied to your arm, and the other you held with your hand. When you wanted to send the rock toward a target you swung the leather bowl on its leather straps over your head, and then you let go of the one strap that wasn't tied. The swinging gathered strength, which is called centrifugal force. When you let go of the strap, the snap sent the rock hurling through space, packing a powerful punch. If the rock was big enough and you swung the sling fast enough, you could hurt or even kill the person or animal you aimed at.

David was very good with the sling. He knew just when to let go of the strap and his pebble always landed where he wanted it to. He would practice on trees and boulders. He liked to hear the pinging sound when his pebble hit its target.

When he spotted a mountain lion stalking his sheep, he would load his sling with a small rock and send it flying in the lion's direction. He always aimed for the animal's backside, because he didn't want to kill it. After all, the lion was just hungry. David wanted to scare it away so the wild beast would look for dinner someplace else.

One evening, as he was playing his harp and dreaming of going into battle, he heard a frantic *baa, baa, baa*. He stood up—the bleating was coming from the far end of the pasture. He grabbed his sling and ran in the direction of the sound. In the moonlight he saw a mountain lion trying to drag a sheep into the forest. Quickly, David loaded his sling with a sizeable rock and let it fly. It hit the beast's flank, and with a howl, the lion let go of the sheep.

David ran to the rescue. The sheep was lying on the ground, but it was alive. When David started talking to it, the sheep opened its eyes and struggled to its feet. David laughed. "Okay, little one, you had a scare. Now quick run to your friends!" The sheep scurried off, and David said a silent prayer, thanking God for helping him. It had been a close call. He almost lost the sheep.

He started to return to his campsite, when he heard snarling behind him. Slowly, he turned around. The lion had come back. He was standing there at the edge of the field staring at David.

I've seen lions on movie sets, and they sure are huge and have big teeth. If I ever saw a lion out of a cage and standing there looking at me, I think I'd run away as fast as I could, I'd be so scared.

But David didn't blink an eye. Quickly, he loaded his sling. With a loud roar, the lion pounced, the force of his powerful muscles carrying him directly toward David. But just as fast, David sent a large rock flying. The rock hit the lion as he was leaping at David and struck him with great force in the head. David ducked as the huge body came tumbling down to the ground.

Frozen, David waited for the lion to rise and pounce again. It lay very still, it's large white fangs opened. It was dead.

David felt sad. He was sorry that he had to kill the lion. It was such a beautiful wild cat. It could have lived a long life. He wished the lion had just run off and left him alone. But he had to protect himself.

He sat down with his harp and wrote a song:

> *Whoever takes God for his refuge,*
> *The Most High as his shelter,*
> *No harm will befall him . . .*
> *For the Lord will order His angels*
> *To guard you wherever you go.*

One day, his father, Jesse, came to visit him.

"David," his father said, "you've been here all alone with the sheep for a long time."

"Oh, I don't mind," David said.

"I know you don't. You are a good son. But just for a break, I want you to go down to Elah Valley, where your brothers are fighting, and check on them."

David's eyes lit up. "Can I go and fight too?"

"Now, now," his father admonished. "I didn't say anything about fighting. All I said was go to visit your brothers. I will send a package of bread and cheese for them. I'm sure they are tired of army food by now. They will appreciate some treats."

Now if you ask me, they'd probably have liked

some ice cream. Bread and cheese doesn't sound like such a treat. But maybe they didn't have ice cream in those days either, and for sure they didn't have freezers to keep it from melting.

David's dad packed up the basket of food for the brothers, and David packed up his harp and sling and off he went. He was very excited. Wow—maybe he'd get to see a battle. That would be great fun.

As he got near Elah Valley—the site of the most recent confrontation with the Philistines—he could see the smoke from the campfires rising in the distance, and soon he could see a field of tents. There were thousands of them. Would he be able to find his brothers in such a large army?

When he approached the encampment, two guards wearing helmets and holding spears stopped him, but when they saw it was just a little kid with a package of food, they let him pass.

David walked around between the tents looking for his brothers, but the soldiers were off in the battlefield. Someone directed him to their tent where he left the food package. But he couldn't just wait for them to return; he had to see what was going on. He had never seen a battle before.

Finally, he reached the site. It amazed him. The

opposing forces were facing each other from two hill-sides on either side of an empty valley. On the one side, the Philistines. On the other side, the Israelites. But nobody was fighting.

"What's going on?" David asked one of the soldiers in the back row. "When does the battle begin?"

"Be quiet," the soldier said. "He will come out at any moment."

"'He'?" David was puzzled. "Who is 'he'?"

"Shhh, you'll see."

But David was very small and couldn't see a thing behind all those soldiers. So he squeezed his way to the front. Now he could see into the valley.

Just then, a trumpet sounded from the Philistine side. And from the enemy ranks stepped out a man like David had never seen before.

He was huge! A giant. Nine feet tall. He was bigger

then Shaquille O'Neal, who is only seven feet. I once stood next to Shaquille O'Neal and I had to crane my neck to look at him. He sure is huge! So this guy had to be humongous.

The giant was a fearsome sight. He had a mean face with deep black eyes and a black beard. On his head he wore a pointy copper helmet, and his whole body was covered in an iron suit.

This was a special armor suit that the Philistines perfected. The suit was made from interlocking iron rings—for strength and flexibility—and the rings in turn were covered with many small metal plates that looked like fish scales.

I asked my mother to get me a suit like that for my birthday, but I never got it.

As if that wasn't enough, the giant wore a huge sword on his belt and carried a spear twice the size of David.

He bellowed in a voice that sounded like thunder, "YOU STINKING ISRAELITE COWARDS—COME OUT AND FIGHT!"

At his words, the Israelite soldiers trembled. David didn't understand why they were so scared.

"Who is this guy?" he asked a soldier near him.

"That's Goliath," the man said in a voice filled with awe.

"Isn't somebody going to fight him?"

"Huh? Look at his size!" exclaimed the soldier. "He is a killer."

Meanwhile, Goliath was just getting warmed up. "YOU ARE ALL SCARED OF ME!" he yelled. "I DARE YOU! COME OUT AND FIGHT ME! IF YOU WIN, WE WILL BE YOUR SLAVES." And then he roared, "BUT IF I WIN—HA, HA, HA." He laughed. "THEN ALL OF YOU WILL BE OUR SLAVES."

There was a fearful murmur from the Israelites, but no one answered him.

He laughed even louder. "HA, HA, HA, HA, HA, HA." And the earth seemed to shake. "YOU ARE AS WEAK AS YOUR GOD. YOU AND YOUR GOD ARE NOTHING."

David's eyes widened in amazement. "Somebody has to fight him!" he said loudly. "He is insulting God!"

David's brothers heard him and the oldest, Eliav, came over. He was very angry. "What are you doing here?"

"I came to bring you some food," David explained.

"And who is watching the sheep?"

"Father took care of that, so I could—"

"Just don't be getting any ideas that you came to

join the fighting," Eliav warned him sternly.

"There is no fighting," David observed. "Everyone is just standing around."

"Don't you get smart with me!" Now Eliav was really mad. "You don't understand what's happening here."

"I do too. This Goliath is insulting God, and you guys are doing nothing about it."

"Listen, you pip-squeak," said another brother, Shama, who joined in berating David. "Everything is riding on this battle—if we lose, we will be slaves again like in Egypt. No one dares to make a mistake. So we wait for the right moment."

"How long have you been waiting?" David asked.

"He's been daring us for forty days now," Shama said.

"Forty days?" David was shocked. "Well, if no one will fight him, I will," he proclaimed.

"Yeah, right!" His brothers laughed.

"Yes, I will fight him and I will beat him."

"You better go back home to your sheep."

His brothers sure were nasty. I tell you, after reading about what Joseph's brothers did to him, and about how mean David's brothers were, I was glad I had only sisters.

As the brothers were belittling David, a guard approached them and said to the boy, "You come with me. Orders from the king."

"The king?" David was surprised.

"See that?" His brothers were fuming. "This means trouble. You and your big mouth."

But David paid no attention, and he just followed the guard to the king's tent—the largest tent in the middle of the camp.

Inside, sitting in a large ornately carved wooden chair, was an old man with a gray beard, wearing red robes and a gold crown—King Saul.

When the guard brought David in, the king stared at him in astonishment. "Who is this?"

"Your majesty," the guard replied, "this is the young man who was boasting he would fight Goliath."

The king let out a short laugh, "Oh, so it's a joke." Then his face saddened. "I really thought that, at last, there was a man among the soldiers willing to fight the giant."

David straightened himself, hoping to appear taller. "I will fight him, your majesty."

The king shook his head. "It's nice to hear that a young boy like you is so brave. But we need a champion right now, and we need him fast."

"Your majesty, we don't need a champion, we have God on our side. I know I can win, because God is with me."

"You have not only courage but faith too. That is amazing for one so young. But you have no experience."

"But I do. I have fought lions who tried to kill my sheep and I won."

"You fought lions? And you are still alive?"

"God helped me, your majesty."

The king thought for a long moment and then he said, "You are just a lad, but there is something special about you. God must be with you . . ." He sighed. "What can I do? What can I do?"

"Trust in God, your majesty. And let me kill Goliath like I killed the lion."

The king thought for a very long time. David wondered if maybe he was praying silently. Then the king said, "All right, I will send you out against Goliath. I have no one else." He turned to the guard. "Send in my generals."

When the generals were informed that the king was sending a little boy against Goliath, they were stunned, and they protested loudly. "Your majesty, this cannot be. We have too much at stake here. We could be enslaved as a result of this folly."

"I am well aware of the stakes," the king said. "Outfit him for battle."

The guards brought in a suit of armor for David. They helped him put it on. But it was heavy and too big for little David. He almost crumpled under the weight of it, and when he tried to walk, the metal clanged loudly as his elbows banged against his sides. The guard helped him put on a helmet, but it was too big—it just bent his ears and dropped to his nose. He couldn't see a thing.

"Maybe Goliath will die laughing," one of the generals scoffed.

"You're right," the king sighed. "It's hopeless."

David spoke up, "Your majesty, I cannot go like this. I have to take off all this metal. I will face this giant like I faced the lion—with my sling. God will protect me better than any iron ever could."

The king studied little David. And then he patted the boy on the head, "Go, and may God bless you."

David left everything behind, even the sword they had given him. He took with him only his shepherd's sling and his pouch into which he placed five smooth stones that he found on the way. He was ready.

That's how he walked out toward Goliath.

When the giant saw David, he blinked twice. Coming toward him was a little kid with a little purse. His laughter rumbled like thunder in the valley. "HA, HA, HA, HA, HA." When he finally stopped laughing, he yelled to David, "COME ON. COME TO ME. I'LL MAKE HAMBURGER OUT OF YOU—A TASTY KIDBURGER!" And then he laughed again, doubling over with mirth.

David just kept walking forward. The closer he got, the bigger Goliath seemed and a knot of fear started to form in his belly. "God is my shepherd," he whispered to himself, "God is with me, God is with me, God is with me . . ."

"HA, HA, HA, HA, HA, HA," the giant bellowed. "IN A MOMENT YOU ALL WILL BE OUR SLAVES!"

David kept advancing.

With a roar, Goliath pulled out his sword and attacked. But the boy deftly skipped away. The sword cracked into a rock, splitting it in half and sending a cloud of dust into the air that for a moment obscured the view.

A hush fell over the Israelite army, and David's brothers were sick with guilt—why hadn't they stopped David from going out to get killed. Above the cloud of dust, they could see the vicious head of Goliath bobbing up and down as he swung his sword for a second time. Could little David still be alive? They held their breath.

But then, they saw a nimble David skipping away. A sigh of relief went up from the Israelites.

Now, really irritated, Goliath raised his sword over his head again and lumbered toward his little enemy.

Calmly, David removed a smooth stone from his shepherd's pouch. He placed it in the leather bowl of his sling, took one step back, and swung the sling over his head. He sent the rock hurling through space, aiming at the only place where Goliath was not protected by armor—straight at the giant's face. It landed exactly where he wanted it to—a perfect shot! The rock hit the giant with such force that it imbedded itself into his forehead.

Goliath let out a howl of agony and fell forward to the ground.

Slowly, ready for the giant to get up again, David approached him. But Goliath wasn't moving. David took the sword from the dead man's grasp. It was very heavy. With two hands he raised it up and brought it down on the giant's neck. Slash! Off came Goliath's head! Now everyone could be sure that he was dead.

This is the part of the story that I always liked best. I know we shouldn't be happy when someone gets killed—it's a terrible thing. But Goliath was such a bully! He was trying to kill little David. Not only that, he wanted to conquer the Israelites and make them slaves.

Of course, the Israelites were happy that they were spared this awful fate. A raucous cheer went up from their side.

The horrified Philistines, who had been grinning happily a second ago, started to run in terror.

With a lot of whooping and hollering, the Israelites, their courage restored, went after them. They chased them all the way back home.

Meanwhile, David's brothers and the generals looked on in awe as David carried the huge head of Goliath—he had to use both hands—and placed it on the ground before King Saul.

The king glanced at the ugly head and turned to David. "We owe you many thanks."

"Don't thank me, your majesty—thank God. Without His help I could never have done it."

Now that's a hero. He didn't even take credit for the victory! Yet, he deserved it. God would have helped anyone who had faith in Him and stood up against Goliath. But *everybody* was too scared. Only David had the courage.

From David we learn to trust in God. It's very important. (If you look at the coins in your pocket, you'll see each one says: IN GOD WE TRUST.) You never know when you will be called upon to do something courageous or extraordinary. If you trust in God now, you will always be ready. Just like David was.

David wanted to hurry home to tell his father what happened, but King Saul had other plans.

First, everybody said a prayer and thanked God for saving them from slavery once again. Then, a great feast was prepared to celebrate the victory. At the feast, King Saul announced that David would become his number one general.

So that's what happened. David became a general, and he was very popular—everybody wanted to serve under him. Later, he married the king's daughter, wrote many more songs, and when King Saul died, he became King David.

His brothers could hardly believe it. Shama went around saying, "If I knew he would become so famous, I would have been nicer to him when he was a kid."

As king, David fought great battles, and in one of those battles, he conquered a pagan city of the Jebusites, which was in the middle of his kingdom. He made it the most famous city in the world—Jerusalem, the capital of Israel—where everyone had faith and trust in God.

Little red-headed David, who had a harp and a sling, and who loved God most of all, became the greatest king the Israelites ever had.

CONCLUSION

DID YOU ENJOY reading some of my favorite stories from the Bible? I hope so. Who knows, maybe someday you too will become a hero!

The Talmud says that when a person has lived for seventy years he has completed a life, and then he starts all over again. So, that means—since I am eighty-two—I am really twelve. Next year, it will be time for my second Bar Mitzvah, because I'll be thirteen again.

And I'll have another chance to be a hero.

But right this minute, I think it's time to go out to play. Are you ready?

Come on, I'll race you. I am running for the playground now and the last one is a rotten egg.

About Kirk Douglas

Kirk Douglas has been a Hollywood legend for over four decades. In a career encompassing more than eighty films, he has earned an Academy Award for a lifetime of achievement and three Academy Award nominations for *Champion*, *The Bad and the Beautiful*, and *Lust for Life*. As an independent producer, he has brought to the screen classics like *Paths of Glory*, *The Vikings*, *Spartacus*, *Lonely Are the Brave*, and *Seven Days in May*. His autobiographies, *Climbing the Mountain: My Search for Meaning* and *The Ragman's Son*, and his three novels, *Dance with the Devil*, *The Gift*, and *Last Tango in Brooklyn*, won praise from critics and became international best-sellers. His first book written for children was *The Broken Mirror*.